*Tibor Gergely's*

# GREAT BIG
# BOOK OF BEDTIME
# STORIES

Tibor Gergely's

BED

# Great Big Book of TIME STORIES

**GOLDEN PRESS • NEW YORK**
Western Publishing Company, Inc.
Racine, Wisconsin

# CONTENTS

Library of Congress Catalog Card Number: 67-20159
ISBN 0-307-16529-9

GOLDEN®, A GOLDEN BOOK® and GOLDEN PRESS® are trademarks of Western Publishing Company, Inc.

# CHRISTOPHER AND THE COLUMBUS

*By Kathryn and Byron Jackson*

EVERY Saturday, rain or shine, hot or cold, snow or blow, Christopher hurried down the city streets to the river. He always got there in time to see the *Columbus* come into the ferryboat slip with a great bumping and tooting and rattling of chains.

The minute he was aboard, Christopher ran up the stairs to see his good friend, Captain McPherson.

Captain McPherson grinned at him and said,

"Fine day for a voyage, Matey!" His parrot whistled happily.

Then Captain McPherson blew the whistle and turned the wheel, and off they started for the other side of the river.

But that wasn't enough for Christopher and the captain. Oh, no! They pretended that the *Columbus* was sailing the real ocean, and was going clear across the world.

They pretended a storm at sea, and a school of sharks, and a treasure island, and a narrow escape from a desperate pirate band.

What wonderful Saturdays they had!

And then came a rainy, blowy, stormy Saturday. Christopher was down at the river earlier than ever. It was so early and so rainy and stormy and blowy, that there was not a single passenger aboard the *Columbus*. Even the crew was still at home and asleep.

"Where will we go today?" Christopher asked.

Captain McPherson rubbed his **chin.** "How about sailing around the Horn?" he said.

"Fine!" cried Christopher.

The parrot screamed, "Chart **your** course, Mates!"

And the *Columbus* started off. Captain McPherson headed straight for **the** ferry slip on the other side.

But the *Columbus* did not go straight across. She went halfway across, and she began to turn.

She turned until she was heading down river—and then she went faster and faster, with a fine streak of white water at her stern.

She scooted right past the wharves and the tall buildings, past big boats and little boats, and under a bridge, and past the Navy Yard, and past the beaches and the marsh grass and the bell buoys and the lighthouse. And there she was, out in the open sea!

The salt wind blew, and the sea gulls sailed by, and a big fish leaped, and for all Christopher knew they might be headed for a real desert island.

11

"Land, ho!" cried the parrot at last.

The land was a narrow strip of island that seemed to be getting narrower all the time.

And there were three little boys on it, waving their shirts and shouting for help.

"Here's a fine howdy-do!" cried Captain McPherson. "Castaways! And very young ones at that! And the *Columbus* can't go in to that reef!"

Christopher didn't answer. He was too busy getting all the life-belts on the ferryboat.

Captain McPherson shouted, "Good lad! Toss them to the castaways!"

Christopher did. He aimed very carefully, and three life-belts landed right on the sand bar.

"Put them on and swim out!" he called.

The castaways heard him. Before long all three of them were bobbing in the

13

ocean near the *Columbus*. Captain McPherson let down a rope ladder. And the three cold, dripping little boys climbed aboard.

"We made a raft yesterday, and went to sea," they said. "But the raft came apart. We were marooned all night!"

Christopher wrapped the castaways in Captain McPherson's big, warm coat. And the *Columbus* started home.

Christopher looked at the three little boys, who were soon half asleep. "They were in bad trouble, weren't they, Captain?" he asked.

Captain McPherson nodded his head.

"We may be in trouble ourselves," he said. "We missed three trips, and I shouldn't be one bit surprised if somebody says, 'McPherson, you can't be captain of the *Columbus* ever any more!'"

Now the *Columbus* was chugging past

the lighthouse. She went past the marsh grass and the beaches, and lots of big and little boats all hurrying out to sea. Then she went under the bridge.

There were crowds of people on the bridge, and crowds of people lined up along the wharves.

"Looks like a holiday!" cried the castaways. They ran out on deck. And the minute those three little boys appeared, it was like a holiday. All the people started to shout and wave and throw down bits of paper.

"There are the lost boys!" they cheered. "The ferryboat found them! The ferryboat rescued them! Hurray for the *Columbus!*"

Captain McPherson smiled a wide smile. Christopher sighed with relief. And ever after that the *Columbus* stayed right in the river, which is a very good place for a river ferryboat to be.

# A DAY
# IN THE JUNGLE

### By Janette Sebring Lowrey

A LITTLE gray mouse crept out of the woods, shivering and sighing and shaking all over with fear.

"Now, now!" said the squirrel, who heard him. "Things aren't as bad as all that!"

"Yes, they are," said the mouse. "In my house by the water hole there's someone who mumbles to himself and moves around, and I'm afraid to go in!"

"Come along," said the squirrel. "We'll give him what for!"

So the mouse and the squirrel set out for the water hole. But on their way they met a hare.

"Come with us to the mouse's house by the water hole," said the squirrel. "There's someone inside who mumbles and moans and pushes things around. We're going to give him what for!"

"I'll do that," said the hare.

So the mouse and the squirrel and the hare set out for the water hole together. But they had not gone far when they met a wolf.

"Don't be frightened, my friends," said the wolf. "I've just had my dinner. But where are you going in such a hurry?"

"We're on our way to the mouse's house by the water hole," said the hare. "There's someone inside who moans and

"Excuse me!" said the antelope, starting off in the opposite direction.

"Come along, my dear," said the wolf. "We're on our way to the mouse's house by the water hole. We're going to give a dreadful creature that's inside what for!"

"But what could *I* do?" the antelope wanted to know.

"Think of your sharp hoofs," said the wolf. "And, by the way, don't be frightened. I've had my dinner."

So the mouse and the squirrel and the hare and the wolf and the antelope

groans and pushes the furniture around. We're going to give him what for! But *you're* not invited."

"Oh, yes," said the wolf, "I can chase him for you."

"Come along, then," said the hare. "But see that you behave yourself."

So the mouse and the squirrel and the hare and the wolf set out for the water hole together.

But they had gone only a few steps when they met an antelope.

set out for the water hole together. But a short distance down the path they met a black panther.

"Don't be frightened, my friends," said the panther. "I've had my dinner. But where are you going in such a hurry?"

"We're on our way to the mouse's house by the water hole," said the antelope. "There's someone inside who moans

"But what could *I* do?" the camel wanted to know.

"Think of your strong legs and your teeth," said the panther. "And, by the way, don't be frightened. We've had our dinner."

So the mouse and the squirrel and the hare and the wolf and the antelope and the panther and the camel set out for the water hole together. But before they had gone very far, they met a rhinoceros.

"I can hear you," said the rhinoceros, "but I can't see you very well. Where are you going in such a hurry?"

"We're going to the Mouse's house by the water hole," said the camel. "There's a horrible monster inside that moans and groans and shrieks and roars and howls and screams and is chopping up the furniture and throwing it out of the window. We're going to give him what for!"

"But *you're* not invited," added the wolf and the black panther.

"Oh, yes," said the rhinoceros. "I am,

and groans and howls and pushes the furniture around. We're going to give him what for! But *you're* not invited!"

"Oh, yes," said the panther. "I can climb in the windows and get him out for you."

"Come along, then," said the antelope. "But see that you behave yourself."

So off they went through the woods: the mouse and the squirrel and the hare and the wolf and the antelope and the black panther. But they had not gone far when they met a camel who was spending his vacation in the jungle.

"Excuse me!" said the camel, starting off in the opposite direction.

"Come along, my dear," said the panther. "We're on our way to the mouse's house by the water hole. We're going to give a terrible monster that's inside what for!"

too. I'm going to the water hole anyway to wade in the water and wallow in the mud."

"Very well, then," said the wolf and the panther and the camel. "But see that you behave yourself."

And off they went, then: the mouse and the squirrel and the hare and the wolf and the antelope and the black panther and the camel and the rhinoceros, through the woods and on their way to the water hole. But before they had gone far they met a giraffe.

"Excuse me!" said the giraffe, starting off in the opposite direction.

"Come along, my dear," said the wolf and the panther. "We're on our way to the mouse's house by the water hole to give a horrible, terrible monster inside what for!"

"But what could I do?" the giraffe wanted to know.

"Think of your long neck," said the panther. "And, by the way, don't be frightened. We've had our dinner."

So the mouse and the squirrel and the hare and the wolf and the antelope and the panther and the camel and the rhinoceros and the giraffe set out together once more. But just around the next turn, they met a brown bear.

"Don't be frightened, my friends," said the brown bear. "I've had my dinner. But where are you going in such a hurry?"

"We're going to the mouse's house by the water hole," said the giraffe. "There's a horrible, terrible monster inside that moans and groans and howls and shrieks and roars and screams and is chopping

21

up the furniture and throwing it out of the window. We're going to give him what for! But *you're* not invited."

"Oh, yes," said the brown bear. "If someone will chase him out, I'll hug him so tightly that he can't get away."

So off they went once more, but just a few steps down the path they met a lion and a tiger.

"Don't be frightened, my friends," said the lion and the tiger. "We've had our dinner. But where are you going?"

"We're on our way to give a horrible, terrible monster what for!" said the bear. "But *you're* not invited."

"Oh, yes we are, too," said the lion and the tiger. "We will invite ourselves."

But they hadn't gone far before they met an elephant.

"Come along," said the lion and the tiger. "There's a terrible, horrible, monstrous ogre in the mouse's house by the water hole. He moans and groans and howls and shrieks and roars and screams. And besides he is chopping up the furniture, throwing it out of the window, and is getting ready to pull the house down about his ears. We're going to give him what for!"

"I'm always ready for a bit of fun," said the elephant.

So off they went together, the mouse and the squirrel and the hare and the wolf and the antelope and the panther

and the camel and the rhinoceros and the giraffe and the bear and the lion and the tiger and the elephant.

And when they came to the water hole, there was a crocodile, resting his chin on the mossy green bank.

"We've come to give the terrible, horrible monster what for!" said the elephant to the crocodile.

"What monster?" the crocodile asked.

"Why, we don't know," said the lion and the tiger. "What monster, mouse?"

"Oh, he's inside," said the mouse, beginning to weep again. "Shake the tree that holds my house, and he'll come out."

So the elephant wrapped his trunk around the trunk of the tree and shook it. And the lion and the tiger and the panther and the wolf and the bear roared and howled and barked and screeched. The giraffe and the antelope and the camel stamped on the ground. The squirrel and the hare got ready to jump.

24

And after a long minute, something small and gray and soft and sleepy flew out of the mouse's house and sat on the limb of the tree next door.

"Who-oo-oo!" said the soft, gray, sleepy creature. "Who-oo? Oh, it's you-oo-oo!" And away he flew.

"Why it was nothing but an owl!" said the elephant, waving his trunk in a surprised sort of way. "Dear me!"

But the lion and the tiger and the bear and the panther and the wolf began to lick their lips with their long, red tongues. "It's nearly time for supper, my friends," they said.

And, in the twinkling of an eye, there wasn't a creature to be seen except the elephant and the rhinoceros, who had stepped into the water hole to wade in the water and wallow in the mud. And

the crocodile was still resting his chin on the bank, of course.

But the little gray mouse had crept quietly into his house.

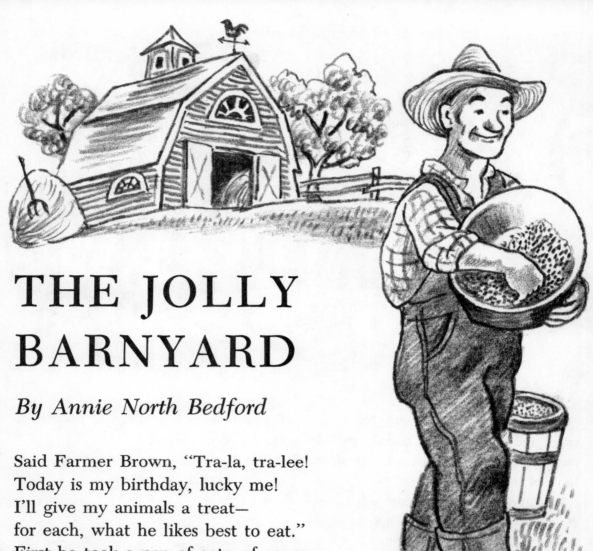

# THE JOLLY BARNYARD

## By Annie North Bedford

Said Farmer Brown, "Tra-la, tra-lee!
Today is my birthday, lucky me!
I'll give my animals a treat—
for each, what he likes best to eat."
First he took a pan of oats, of course,
to the baby colt and the mother horse.
For the cow and calf he set corn down.
" 'Cause today is my birthday," said Farmer Brown.
The big white ram and the fat black sheep
ate all the grain in a great big heap.
The gobbling turkey ate and ate until
he had to admit he'd eaten his fill.
The chickens and rooster got their food—
enough for all their hungry brood.
And so did the duck, and so did the drake,
and the ducklings down beside the lake.

The dog got bones to bury and to chew.
The cat got milk—and the kitten did, too.
When all the animals had been fed,
Farmer Brown left, and the spotted cow said,
"Kind Farmer Brown! What would you say
we could do for him on his birthday?"

"We'll pull his loads smoothly, with never a jolt,"
said the big brown horse and her little brown colt.

"Moo-oo, I'll give him lots of milk," said the cow.
Said her calf, "I will, too, some day, somehow!"

"Baa-aa,
we'll give him wool,"
said the sheep.
"For our fleece is soft
and warm and deep."

"Gobble!"
said the turkey.
"As well as I
am able,
I'll decorate his
Thanksgiving table."

"Cluck! I will give
him eggs,"
said the hen.
Said the rooster,
"I'll wake him
in the mornings,
then."

"Quack!
He can have
duck eggs,"
said the duck.
"And I'll swim
on his pond,"
said the drake,
"for luck."

"Bow-wow!"
said the dog.
"I'll guard his house
both night and day,
but most of all
when he's away!"

"Mew! We'll catch
his mice,"
said the cat.
"We're good hunters,"
said the kitten.
"Farmer Brown
will tell you that."

And inside the farmhouse waited Mrs. Brown.
She smiled as the farmer sat him down.
"Happy birthday, dear," she said.
"Here is something you'll like to eat—
an extra-special birthday treat!"
"Thank you," said the farmer,
"It's plain to see
what a happy birthday this turned out to be!"

35

# SCUFFY THE TUGBOAT

## (AND HIS ADVENTURES DOWN THE RIVER)

### *By Gertrude Crampton*

SCUFFY was sad. Scuffy was cross. Scuffy sniffed his blue smokestack.

"A toy store is no place for a red-painted tugboat," said Scuffy, and he sniffed his blue smokestack again. "I was meant for bigger things."

And Scuffy lay on his side and would not show his blue smokestack to those who came to buy.

And the man with the polka dot tie, who owned the toy store and Scuffy, sighed to think he had a red-painted

36

tugboat that would not show its fine blue smokestack.

"Perhaps you would not be cross if you went sailing," he said.

So one night the man with the polka dot tie took Scuffy home to his little boy.

He filled the white bathtub with water, half cold and half hot.

"Sail, little tugboat," said the little boy.

Scuffy sniffed his blue smokestack.

"I won't sail in a bathtub," said Scuffy. "I won't! I won't!

"A tub is no place for a red-painted tugboat. I was meant for bigger things."

And when the man with the polka dot tie and his little boy saw that Scuffy

would not sail in the tub, not even down to the faucets, they took the little tugboat out of the water and went off to bed.

"Tomorrow," said the man with the polka dot tie, "we will go to the brook that starts high in the hills. Perhaps our red-painted tugboat will sail tomorrow."

Next day the man with the polka dot tie and his little boy carried Scuffy through two meadows and across a field of green, young corn.

Scuffy could hear a laughing, singing brook, still chuckling over some joke it had heard high in the hills where it started.

"There," said the man with the polka dot tie, and he put Scuffy in the laughing brook. "Sail, little tugboat."

Scuffy floated on a ruffle of the brook, and saw above him the smiling faces of the man with the polka dot tie and his little boy.

But it was Spring, and the brook was full to the brim with its water. And the water moved in a hurry, as all things move in a hurry when it is Spring.

"Come back, little tugboat, come back," cried the little boy as the hurrying, brimful brook carried Scuffy downstream.

"Not I," tooted Scuffy. "Not I. This is the life for me."

All that day Scuffy sailed along with the brook.

Past the meadows filled with cowslips. Past the women washing clothes on the bank. Past the little woods filled with violets.

Cows came to the brook to drink.

They stood in the cool water, and it was fun to sail around between their legs and bump softly into their noses.

It was fun to see them drink.

But when a white and brown cow almost drank Scuffy instead of the brook's cool water, that was not fun!

And there was no rest. For it was Spring, and the brook moved in a hurry, as all things move in a hurry when it is Spring.

The brook flowed into the forest, and deep inside it widened into a pool.

As Scuffy sailed by, he watched a fawn drink at the pool.

A mother skunk and her babies marched along the bank in a fine, straight line.

"This is fun," thought Scuffy. "The man with the polka dot tie has never seen the forest animals come to the pool to drink. I like this river. This is the life for me!"

Late that afternoon Scuffy passed over the rapids.

Here the water was shallow and there were many, many stones. Most of the stones were round and smooth, for the brook had dashed over them and rolled them about for years and years and years.

"But they are still stones and they are still hard," said Scuffy crossly as the brook slapped him across the rapids.

Night came, and with it the moon.

There was nothing to see but the quiet trees, and now and then a farmhouse with shining windows, and once some rabbits with gleaming eyes.

"This is nice," thought Scuffy. "I like night."

But just then a fish nibbled Scuffy's red side and a large and important owl called, "Hoot! Hooooot!"

"Toot, toooot!" cried the frightened

red-painted tugboat, and he wished he could see the smiling face of the man with the polka dot tie.

When morning came and the sun danced on the brook again, Scuffy was cross instead of frightened.

"A brook is no place for a red-painted tugboat," said Scuffy. "I was meant for bigger things."

Around a bend and past a small woods the brook ran, and there was another brook.

"Oh, oh!" said Scuffy. "What happens now? Which way do I want to go?"

But there was only one way to go, and that was with the running water where the two brooks met.

And where their waters ran together, they made a small river. And with the river sailed Scuffy, the red-painted tugboat.

"This is better," said Scuffy. "This is the life for me!" And he sailed happily with the river and felt very important.

All during the day the small river grew and grew, for it was joined by brooks that had come laughing and jumping and bubbling down from high places.

By night the river was quite wide and quite deep, and Scuffy was proud to sail with it.

He was proud when he sailed past villages.

"People build villages at the edge of my river," said Scuffy, and he straightened his blue smokestack.

Once Scuffy's river joined a small one jammed with logs. Here were men in heavy jackets and great boots walking about on the floating logs trying to pry them free.

"Toot, toot, let me through," demanded Scuffy. But the men paid no attention to him. They pushed the logs apart so they would drift with the river to the sawmill in the town. Scuffy bumped along with the jostling logs.

"Ouch!" he cried as two logs bumped together.

"Oooo!" he shouted as he dodged the sharp hook of a man who was helping to swing the logs.

"This is a fine river," said Scuffy, "but it's very busy and very big for me."

He was proud when he sailed under the bridges.

"My river is so wide and so deep that people must build bridges to cross it."

The river moved through big towns now instead of villages.

And the bridges over it were very wide—wide enough so that many cars and trucks and streetcars could cross all at once.

The river got deeper and deeper. Scuffy did not have to tuck up his bottom.

The river moved faster and faster.

"I feel like a train instead of a tugboat," said Scuffy, hurrying along.

He was proud when he passed the old flour mill with its water wheel.

"My river moves so fast and is so strong that it can turn the big water wheel.

42

"Without my river, this miller could not make his flour."

But no one cared what Scuffy thought, and no one heard what Scuffy said. There was only the river, and it was too busy to listen to Scuffy.

The river got wider and wider. Sometimes Scuffy could not see the banks.

Sometimes the sun shone on Scuffy and his great, rushing river. But often the rain fell, too, for it was Spring.

High in the hills and the mountains

CANDY·SODA

the winter snow melted. And all the water had to go somewhere. Some sank into the ground. But the ground could not take it all.

So water ran into the creeks and the brooks, and they ran faster and faster.

As the brooks joined the small rivers, the small rivers ran faster and faster and faster.

As the small rivers joined the great rivers, the great rivers ran faster and faster and faster.

And Scuffy's great river went so fast that it carried Scuffy along every which way—frontwards, and backwards, and half the time sidewards.

"There is too much water in this river," said Scuffy. "Soon the water will splash over the top. And I will splash with it. What a flood there will be!"

Soon great armies of men came to save the fields and the towns and the houses from the rushing water.

They filled bags with sand and put them at the edge of the river.

"They're making higher banks for the river," shouted Scuffy, "to hold the water back."

The water rose higher and higher.

The men built the sand bags higher and higher.

Higher! went the river. Higher! went the sand bags.

At last the water rose no more. The flood water rushed on to the sea and Scuffy raced along with the flood. The people and the fields and the towns were safe.

Around the curves, between the hills, past the towns raced the river and Scuffy. One night they came to a great dam.

The dam was strong and tall, and thick and heavy.

It held Scuffy's river back until the water was strong and powerful.

Then over the dam went the river,

carrying Scuffy with it. The water crowded into the channel, turned heavy water wheels, and made electricity as it went on its way.

But safely down the river sailed Scuffy.

"Think of all the lights," puffed Scuffy, "all the radios, telephones, irons, and vacuum cleaners for miles around that work because we went over the dam."

Oh, it was a busy place and a noisy place! The cranes groaned as they swung the cargoes into great ships. The porters shouted as they carried suitcases and boxes on board.

Horses stamped, and truck motors roared, streetcars clanged and people

shouted. Scuffy said, "Toot, toot," but nobody noticed.

On went the river to the sea. At last Scuffy sailed into a big city. Here the river widened, and all about were docks and wharves.

The whistles blew—policemen's whistles, train whistles, deep whistles from the great ships as the gangplanks were pulled in.

And just beyond lay the sea.

"Oh, oh!" cried Scuffy when he saw the sea. "There is no beginning and there is no end to the sea. I wish I could find the man with the polka dot tie and his little boy!"

Just as the little red-painted tugboat sailed past the last piece of land, a hand reached out and picked him up. And there was the man with the polka dot tie, with his little boy beside him.

"I thought the river would carry you this far, little tugboat," said the man with the polka dot tie. "We have been wating for you."

"The sea is no place for a red-painted tugboat," said Scuffy. "I was meant for *safer* things."

Scuffy is home now.

He sails from one end of the bathtub to the other.

"This is the place for a red-painted tugboat," says Scuffy. "And this is the life for me."

48

# TOOTLE

## By Gertrude Crampton

Far, far to the west of everywhere is the village of Lower Trainswitch. All the baby locomotives go there to learn to be big locomotives. The young locomotives steam up and down the tracks, trying to call out the long, sad *Tooo Ooot* of the big locomotives. But the best they can do is a gay little *Tootle.*

Lower Trainswitch has a fine school for engines. There are lessons in Whistle Blowing, Stopping for a Red Flag Waving, Puffing Loudly When Starting, Coming Around Curves Safely, Screeching When Stopping, and Clicking and Clacking Over the Rails.

Of all the things that are taught in the Lower Trainswitch School for Locomotives, the most important is, of course, Staying on the Rails No Matter What.

The head of the school is an old engineer named Bill. Bill always tells the new locomotives that he will not be angry if they sometimes spill the soup pulling the diner, or if they turn the milk to butter now and then. But they will never, never be good trains unless they get 100 A+ in Staying on the Rails No Matter What. All the baby engines work very hard to get 100 A+ in Staying on the Rails. After a few weeks not one of the engines in the Lower Trainswitch School for Trains would even think of getting off the rails, no matter—well, no matter what.

One day a new locomotive named Tootle came to school.

"Here is the finest baby I've seen since old 600," thought Bill. He patted the gleaming young locomotive and said, "How would you like to grow up to be the Flyer between New York and Chicago?"

"If a Flyer goes very fast, I should like to be one," Tootle answered. "I love to go fast. Watch me."

He raced all around the roundhouse.

"Good! Good!" said Bill. "You must study Whistle Blowing, Puffing Loudly When Starting, Stopping for a Red Flag Waving, and Pulling the Diner without Spilling the Soup.

"But most of all you must study Staying on the Rails No Matter What. Remember, you can't be a Flyer unless you get 100 A+ in Staying on the Rails."

Tootle promised that he would re-

member and that he would work very hard. He did, too.

He even worked hard at Stopping for a Red Flag Waving. Tootle did not like those lessons at all. There is nothing a locomotive hates more than stopping.

But Bill said that no locomotive ever, ever kept going when he saw a red flag waving.

One day, while Tootle was practicing for his lesson in Staying on the Rails No Matter What, a dreadful thing happened.

He looked across the meadow he was running through and saw a fine, strong black horse.

"Race you to the river." shouted the black horse, and kicked up his heels.

Away went the horse. His black tail streamed out behind him, and his mane tossed in the wind. Oh, how he could run!

"Here I go," said Tootle to himself.

"If I am going to be a Flyer, I can't let a horse beat me," he puffed. "Everyone at school will laugh at me."

His wheels turned so fast that they were silver streaks. The cars lurched and bumped together. And just as Tootle was sure he could win, the tracks made a great curve.

"Oh, Whistle!" cried Tootle. "That horse will beat me now. He'll run straight while I take the Great Curve."

Then the Dreadful Thing happened. After all that Bill had said about Staying on the Rails No Matter What, Tootle jumped off the tracks and raced alongside the black horse!

The race ended in a tie. Both Tootle and the black horse were happy. They stood on the bank of the river and talked.

"It's nice here in the meadow," Tootle said.

When Tootle got back to school, he said nothing about leaving the rails. But he thought about it that night in the roundhouse.

"Tomorrow I will work hard," decided Tootle. "I will not even think of leaving the rails, no matter what."

And he did work hard. He practiced tootling so much that the Mayor Himself ran up the hill, his green coattails flapping, and said that everyone in the village had a headache and would he please stop TOOTLING.

So Tootle was sent to practice Staying on the Rails No Matter What.

As he came to the Great Curve, Tootle looked across the meadow. It was full of buttercups.

"It's like a big yellow carpet. How I should like to play in them and hold one under my searchlight to see if I like butter!" thought Tootle. "But no, I am going to be a Flyer and I must practice Staying on the Rails No Matter What!"

Tootle clicked and clacked around the Great Curve. His wheels began to say over and over again, "Do you like butter? Do you?"

"I don't know," said Tootle crossly. "But I'm going to find out."

He stopped much faster than any good Flyer ever does, unless he is stopping for a Red Flag Waving. He hopped off the tracks and bumped along the meadow to the yellow buttercups.

And he danced around and around and held one of the buttercups under his searchlight.

"I do like butter!" cried Tootle. "I do!"

At last the sun began to go down, and it was time to hurry to the roundhouse.

That evening while the Chief Oiler was playing checkers with old Bill, he said, "It's queer. It's very queer, but I found grass between Tootle's front wheels today."

"Hmm," said Bill. "There must be grass growing on the tracks."

"Not on our tracks," said the Day Watchman, who spent his days watching the tracks and his nights watching Bill and the Chief Oiler play checkers.

Bill's face was stern. "Tootle knows he must get 100 A+ in Staying on the Rails No Matter What, if he is going to be a Flyer."

Next day Tootle played all day in the meadow. He watched a green frog and he made a daisy chain. He found a rain barrel, and he said softly, "Toot!" "TOOT!" shouted the barrel. "Why, I sound like a Flyer already!" cried Tootle.

That night the First Assistant Oiler said he had found a daisy in Tootle's bell. The day after that, the Second Assistant Oiler said that he had found hollyhock flowers floating in Tootle's eight bowls of soup.

And then the Mayor Himself said that he had seen Tootle chasing butterflies in the Meadow. The Mayor Himself said that Tootle had looked very silly, too.

Early one morning Bill had a long, long talk with the Mayor Himself.

When the Mayor Himself left the Lower Trainswitch School for Locomotives, he laughed all the way to the village.

"Bill's plan will surely put Tootle back on the track," he chuckled.

Bill ran from one store to the next, buying ten yards of this and twenty yards of that and all you have of the other. The Chief Oiler and the First, Second, and Third Assistant Oilers were hammering and sawing instead of oiling and polishing. And Tootle? Well, Tootle was in the meadow watching the butterflies flying and wishing he could dip and soar as they did.

56

Not a store in Lower Trainswitch was open the next day and not a person was at home. By the time the sun came up, every villager was hiding in the meadow along the tracks. And each of them had a red flag. It had taken all the red goods in Lower Trainswitch, and hard work by the Oilers, but there was a red flag for everyone.

Soon Tootle came tootling happily down the tracks. When he came to the meadow, he hopped off the tracks and rolled along the grass. Just as he was thinking what a beautiful day it was, a red flag poked up from the grass and waved hard. Tootle stopped, for every locomotive knows he must Stop for a Red Flag Waving.

"I'll go another way," said Tootle.

He turned to the left, and up came another waving red flag, this time from the middle of the buttercups.

When he went to the right, there was another red flag waving.

There were red flags waving from the buttercups, in the daisies, under the trees, near the bluebirds' nest, and even one behind the rain barrel. And, of course, Tootle had to stop for each one, for a locomotive must always Stop for a Red Flag Waving.

"Red flags," muttered Tootle. "This meadow is full of red flags. How can I have any fun?"

"Whenever I start, I have to stop. Why did I think this meadow was such a fine place? Why don't I ever see a green flag?"

Just as the tears were ready to slide out of his boiler, Tootle happened to look back over his coal car. On the tracks stood Bill, and in his hand was a big green flag. "Oh!" said Tootle.

He puffed up to Bill and stopped.

"This is the place for me," said Tootle. "There is nothing but red flags for locomotives that get off their tracks."

"Hurray!" shouted the people of Lower Trainswitch, and jumped up from their hiding places. "Hurray for Tootle the Flyer!"

Now Tootle is a famous Two-Miles-a-Minute Flyer. The young locomotives listen to his advice.

"Work hard," he tells them. "Always remember to Stop for a Red Flag Waving. But most of all, Stay on the Rails No Matter What."

# TRAVEL

*By Kathleen N. Daly*

Once upon a time, long ago,
   there was only one way to travel.

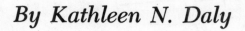
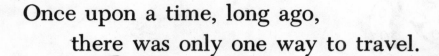

People had to walk, or be
carried by someone else.
   After a long time,
animals were trained
to carry people and their things.
   In some places horses and
oxen were used.

In other places, camels, elephants,
and llamas learned to carry people.

60

The patient donkey and the mule
learned to pull the travois.

In winter, fleet-footed horses
carried people in sleighs.

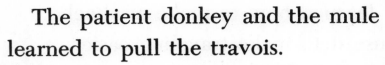

In far northern lands,
dog teams still draw sleds
across the great white snows.

Then man learned how to make a wheel,
and how to use it to make traveling easier.
The first wheels were used
on carts and chariots and wheelbarrows.

Through the years, men built
wagons and carriages and coaches.
All of these helped people to go places
and to move their things.
Travel was becoming easier and faster.

The first boats that men made
were the raft and the canoe.

The raft was made
by tying logs together.

Men cut a long hollow place
in a log, and it was a canoe.

Much later, sailors discovered
how the wind could help them,
and they made sailing ships.

When the wind didn't blow hard enough,
there were many oarsmen to row the boat.

Still later ships,
such as the speedy clippers,
were driven entirely by the wind.

One day a ship was built
which did not even have sails.
It was driven by steam.
The first steamboats were not very fast.
But in time people learned more and more
about steam power.

Today there are many kinds of ships,
and most of them use oil to make them go.
There are huge ocean liners,
and fussy little tugboats.

There are cargo ships and fireboats,
cruisers and battleships,
ferry boats and river boats
and submarines.

How many do you know?

On land, too, people learned how to use steam power.

And railroad trains were built.

What an adventure it was to ride on one of the first trains— and quite a dangerous one, too!

Today, fast trains will take you almost anywhere you want to go— over rivers and lakes, through tunnels in the mountainside, and right across a country from one coast to the other.

Wheels, wheels, turning, turning—
always going farther, always going faster.
Always man wanted more speed.
He made a horseless carriage.
It was rather funny, and it was not very fast.
Roads were rough and muddy or dusty.
Tires punctured easily.

There were no repair shops.
No service stations to buy gasoline.
But cars improved year by year.
Great highways were built.
Now auto buses carry people
wherever they want to go.

70

And there are taxis in towns.
Trucks and vans carry things.
There are fire engines
to rush to fires.
And ambulances to carry
sick people to hospitals.

From earliest times men had dreamed
of flying like birds.

At last some brave men
tried to fly in balloons,
and in gliders,
and in dirigibles,
to make their dreams
come true.

At last the airplane which flew
with motor and fuel was invented.
As man's skill with airplanes grew,
he learned how to fly higher and faster,
and much longer distances.

Pilots learned how to take off
and land in a tiny space,
in the wingless helicopter.

They learned how to fly faster
than sound can travel,
in a jet-propelled plane.
   One day, perhaps man
will be able to travel to the moon—
and beyond—in rockets.
   And who knows! Perhaps *you* will!

# LITTLE RED RIDING HOOD

## *Told by Elsa Jane Werner*

ONCE upon a time there was a sweet little girl whom everyone loved, most of all her mother and grandmother. Wherever she went, this little girl wore a little red cape with a red hood, so her friends came to call her Red Riding Hood.

One day little Red Riding Hood's mother said to her, "How would you like to go to see your grandmother today?"

Of course Red Riding Hood was delighted, so her mother packed a little basket with custard and jelly, a loaf of fine white bread and a bottle of red wine, for Red Riding Hood's grandmother had not been feeling well.

Red Riding Hood put on her little cape and hood, and her mother kissed her good-by, and said to her, "Now be sure to go straight to your grandmother's, and do not stop to play or talk to any strangers in the woods."

Red Riding Hood promised to be careful, and off she started. She loved the walk through the shady green woods, where shy little flowers peeped out from beds of ferns and bright-eyed squirrels and bunnies skipped along beside her in the friendliest way.

But today she did not stop to play with any of her forest friends. She kept right on the path.

Suddenly from behind a big oak tree appeared a great gray wolf. He was an evil-looking fellow, but he smiled at little Red Riding Hood and said politely,

"Good morning, my dear. And where are you going all alone?"

"My grandmother is sick and I am going to her little cottage in the woods to take her this basket from my mother," said little Red Riding Hood. "And my mother says I am not to stop to play along the way or speak to strangers."

"Always obey your mother, my dear," said the wolf, eyeing Red Riding Hood hungrily. "Now I do not want to delay you, since you have a long way to go, so good day!"

With a little bow the wolf disappeared among the trees, and Red Riding Hood skipped along the path toward her grandmother's house.

The wicked wolf lost no time. He took a short cut through the woods and reached the grandmother's cottage long before little Red Riding Hood.

"Who is there?" called the grandmother, who was still in bed.

"It is I, little Red Riding Hood," said the wolf, trying to make his voice sound soft and sweet.

"Come in, my dear," said the grandmother. "Just pull the latchstring."

So the wolf pulled the latchstring and slipped into the grandmother's cottage, and he ate her up in one big bite. Then he put on her nightgown and nightcap and climbed into her bed. He was just pulling the sheet up over his nose when Red Riding Hood rapped at the door.

"Who is there?" called the wolf, trying to make his voice sweet and quavery.

"It is I, little Red Riding Hood," said the little girl.

"Come in, my dear," said the wolf. "Just pull the latchstring."

So Red Riding Hood went in and put her little basket down on the table.

"Now come closer, my dear," said the wolf.

"Why, Granny, what big ears you have!" cried Red Riding Hood as she walked up to the bed.

"The better to hear you with, my dear," said the wolf.

"And Granny, what big eyes you have!" cried Red Riding Hood.

"The better to see you with, my dear," said the wolf.

"And Granny, what big teeth you have!"

"The better to EAT you with!" snapped the wolf, springing at Red Riding Hood.

Calling for help, the little girl ran out of the cottage and straight into the arms of a sturdy woodcutter.

He stepped into the house and with one blow of his axe killed the wicked wolf. Then he slit him open, and out stepped Red Riding Hood's grandmother, none the worse for her fright.

She kissed Red Riding Hood warmly, and thanked the woodcutter for saving their lives. Then, after they had all had a nice lunch from little Red Riding Hood's basket, the woodcutter took the little girl home.

There has never been another wolf seen in that forest, but little Red Riding Hood takes no chances. She keeps right on the path, does not stop to play along the way, and never speaks to strangers.

# LITTLE GRAY DONKEY

## By Alice Hunt

"OH DEAR," brayed Little Gray Donkey. "I'm so tired of being by myself!"

Little Gray Donkey lived all alone in a field on the edge of a wood. Sometimes he ran about the field, but most of the day he stood quite still, nibbling grass and thinking how nice it would be if he had a friend of his own.

When the farmer came to see him, Little Gray Donkey would try to tell him all about it, but the farmer never seemed to understand. He just scratched Little Gray Donkey's head and patted him before going away again.

Now this day Little Gray Donkey was leaning over the hedge, watching the rabbits playing in the wood, and it made him feel more lonely than ever.

He saw that Father Rabbit was carrying a bunch of carrots, and behind him came three little rabbits.

The first was carrying a nice fresh lettuce.

The second had his paws full of radishes.

And the third held a beautiful bouquet of dandelions.

Last of all came Mother Rabbit, gently holding a rhubarb leaf on which she had arranged some wild strawberries.

Little Gray Donkey's mouth watered. "Hee-haw!" he sighed. "I do believe they're having a party. I believe," he brayed softly to himself, "I believe I could push my way into the wood."

He pushed and pushed, and though the hedge was thick and prickly, he took no notice of the prickles. At last

Father Rabbit and Mother Rabbit and their three children were scurrying to and fro, looking very pleased and excited.

Suddenly Little Gray Donkey noticed that they were carrying bundles. Father Rabbit popped into the family burrow, and the others followed him.

Then they all came out of the back door with their paws empty, and away they scampered to find something else.

Little Gray Donkey watched them.

he was through, and he moved slowly and softly towards the rabbits' front door.

As he bent his head to listen, he heard a thud, thud, and knew that one of the rabbits was knocking with its hind legs on the floor of the burrow, to warn the others that a stranger was near by.

"I suppose I'm spoiling their party. I suppose I'd better go away," said Little Gray Donkey sadly.

After a time he saw two long ears sticking up above the ferns; Father Rabbit had come out the back door, and was watching him.

Little Gray Donkey lifted his head. "I only wanted to watch your party, but I'll go away if you'd like me to," he brayed.

Father Rabbit disappeared, but presently Little Gray Donkey was startled by a voice—coming from somewhere about his ankles—saying, "Perhaps you would be so kind as to take one step backwards."

Little Gray Donkey backed away from the door of the burrow, and sat down. Out came Mother Rabbit with strawberries and a pile of beech leaves.

Out came the little rabbits with carrots, lettuce, radishes, and dandelions.

And out came Father Rabbit with cabbage leaves, onions, and lots of other good things.

Having arranged the food on a patch of grass outside the burrow, the rabbits sat in a semicircle, and Mother Rabbit placed a beech leaf piled with strawberries in front of Little Gray Donkey.

He was sure it was the first time any-one had given a donkey strawberries, and it was as much as he could do to bray his thanks.

Just as he was about to start on the strawberries, they were whisked away from under his nose! The rabbits grabbed everything, and scuttled back into their burrow.

Little Gray Donkey sat there, disap-pointed and dismayed. He couldn't un-derstand it.

"Hey, what are you doing there?" demanded a voice he knew very well.

He jumped to his feet, and saw the farmer pushing his way through the gap in the hedge.

Little Gray Donkey knew it was useless to try to explain, so he let the farmer lead him back to the field.

But he just could not bear to watch while the farmer mended the gap with branches and wire. Even after the farmer had gone away, Little Gray Donkey stood with his back to the wood, his head hanging.

Suddenly, Little Gray Donkey felt that someone was watching him. He turned around—and there on the grass lay the cabbage leaves, the onions, the radishes, the carrots, the lettuce, the dandelions, and six beech leaves piled with strawberries. There in a semicircle sat Father Rabbit, Mother Rabbit, and the three little rabbits.

Little Gray Donkey is never lonely now. Every day, the three little rabbits come to play with him, and more often than not Father Rabbit and Mother Rabbit come with them.

# FIVE LITTLE FIREMEN

### By Margaret Wise Brown and Edith Thacher Hurd

A LITTLE HOUSE caught on fire.

The fire started so quietly, and it was such a little fire at first.

A flame like a little mouse came darting in and out of a hole in the hall closet and darted back again. A policeman smelled it.

So he ran to the corner, opened the red alarm box and called the Fire Department. Then he went back to the house.

Ding, ding, ding,
rings the alarm in the fire station.

Ding, ding, ding—
Five little firemen slide down the firehouse pole.

"Sparks!" shouts the First Little Fireman.

He puts on his white helmet, twirls his black mustache, and jumps into the little red Chief's car with its shiny brass bell. Cling, clang!

The First Little Fireman has to be the first at the fire, to tell all the other firemen what to do when they get there.

He is the Fire Chief.

"A fire won't wait," says the Second Little Fireman. Round as a pumpkin, he jumps into the driver's seat of the hook-and-ladder truck, the biggest fire engine of all.

"We'll save all the people," says the Third Little Fireman.

The Third Little Fireman jumps on the side of the hook-and-ladder truck as it rolls out the door. He has muscles as big as baseballs, he is that strong. He runs up the ladders and carries the people down the ladders—that Third Little Fireman.

"We'll squirt lots of water," says the Fourth Little Fireman, who is bright as a button and so drives the huge tower truck.

"I sneeze in the smoke," says the Fifth Little Fireman. Spry as a fly, he jumps on his hose truck and roars out the firehouse door.

Clang, clang, clang, whoooooo, wheeeeee.

Get out of the way!
Get out of the way!
Here come
the Five Little Firemen.
With a clang, cling, clang,
  and a Wheeeeeeeee
  and a Whoooooooooooooooooooooo
they go whizzing up a street called

Oak Street
then whizzing
  around a corner
    into 12½ Street
down Asphalt Avenue
and up the King's Highway
and over Baseball Boulevard
to Small Bush Road.
  Dong, dong, dong.

So Mrs. Hurricane Jones, still very sleepy, threw her mirrors out the window and picked up her pillow and ran downstairs.

Mr. Hurricane Jones grabbed his pipe and his matches and came afterwards to be sure that all his family were out of the house and standing in a line on the lawn.

And there they were, all safely out on their front lawn, each holding in his arms what he loved most.

And there on Small Bush Road was the little house on fire.

Flames the size of pocket handkerchiefs were waving out of the windows. And lots of smoke!

This was the house of the Hurricane Jones Family, and inside they were sleepily sneezing with smoke.

"House on fire! Get out! As quick as you can. Step lively!" said the policeman.

Mrs. Hurricane Jones tried to grab her three little boys and run out of the house with them; but when she went to grab them, the first little boy had run to grab his cat, the second little boy had run downstairs and out of the house to take care of his rabbits, and the third little boy had grabbed all the flowers that he had picked the day before and was halfway down the stairs with them.

The First Fireman shouts orders.

The Third Fireman rushes off to find the cook.

The Second Fireman backs the hook-and-ladder truck into just the right place. The Hurricane Jones's house is too tiny for big ladders. So he takes one of the little ladders and puts it up to the side of the house.

The Fourth Little Fireman points the water tower at the flames and squirts.

And the Fifth Little Fireman unrolls the hose and screws it onto the red fire hydrant.

The water that runs under the street in big pipes all the time gushes through the hose.

It squirts out of the nozzle like a roaring river through the air. Sh-sh-sh-sh!

Swishhsh—they smash in the windows to let out the smoke.

And swishhsh—in roars the water to put out the flames.

The smoke gets all brown and yellow when the water hits it.

They chop down the burning wood and throw fireproof blankets over the furniture.

But where is the jolly fat cook?

The Third Little Fireman has found the cook and he wants to carry her down the ladder on his back in the fireman's carry. "Nix," says she.

She is too fat to carry and too big to jump into a net and too jolly to stay and burn up in the flames.

So they shoot up the life-line for the Hurricane Jones's jolly fat cook to slide down.

And down she comes.

"Jewallopers!" says she. "It was getting warm up there."

93

And soon all the bright flames were wet black ashes.

And the crackling sound of the flames was quiet and there was only the great purring of the red hose truck pumping water and the bright searchlights of the fire engines making the trees and the bushes much greener than they had been before. The fire was over, and the Hurricane Jones Family went home with their Uncle Clement to sleep.

"Fire's out," calls the Chief.

"Let's go," says the Second Little Fireman.

"Some cook!" says the Third Little Fireman.

The engines turn around and go away. Only their bells clang slowly now, Clang, Cling, Clong,
    and a ding, ding, ding, they all go back to the firehouse.

The Five Little Firemen have to wash the engines. They polish the bells and sirens and all their equipment to be ready for another fire alarm at any minute, should one come. But there is no other fire that night.

Five Sleepy Firemen jump into bed.

Five Little Firemen,
Brave as can be,
Sleep, and they dream
of the beautiful sea.

That hurry along
When they hear the gong
And the Whoooo
And the Wheeeee
And the ding, ding, dong—
These are all things

SONG

Flames and smoke
And the glass that broke
And the fires that rise
Into the skies
And scorch the stars
And motor cars

To sing about.
O yes, O no.
There is no doubt,

The finest fire
Is the fire that's out.
Good night.

# ANIMAL GYM

*By Beth Greiner Hoffman*

Things would be in an awful fuss if . . .
. . . animals had gym with us.

Oh, how funny it would seem—
Elephants—walking the balance beam!

Toss a ball
And up it goes—
A seal would catch it
On his nose.

101

# Monkeys on the kiddie-climb

Think of new tricks all the time.

The lion's tail makes a jump that's fine:
One, two, three, four, everyone in line.
We could never, ever, hope
To beat a tiger up the rope.

# Tell me now if you know who

Jumps hurdles like the kangaroo.

Yes, things would be
In an awful fuss,

# If animals had gym with us!

# THE TAXI THAT HURRIED

*By Lucy Sprague Mitchell, Irma Simonton Black, and Jessie Stanton*

ONCE there was a taxi. It was a bright yellow taxi with two red lines running around its body. It had a soft leather seat and two hard little let-down seats.

It was a smart little taxi. For it could start fast—jerk-whizz!! It could tear along the street—whizz-squeak!! It could stop fast—squeak-jerk!!

Its driver's name was Bill. He stepped on the gas to make the taxi start fast. He stepped on the brake to make it stop fast. Together they were a speedy pair. They could wiggle through the traffic, they could jiggle up the passengers better than anything else on the city streets.

One day the taxi was standing on the street close to the sidewalk. Bill and the little taxi didn't like to stand still long. They liked to keep on the move. "I wonder who will be our next passengers," thought Bill.

Just then Bill heard some feet running on the sidewalk, thump, thump, thump! And he heard some smaller feet pattering along, too, thumpety, thumpety, thumpety! He leaned out and saw Tom with a little suitcase and Tom's mother with a big suitcase. And both of them were breathing hard.

"Oh!" gasped Tom's mother. "Taxi driver-man, please drive us to the station as fast as you can. We're very late and the train won't wait. Oh!—oh!—oh!"

Tom and his mother tumbled into the taxi and slammed the door.

"Sure, lady," answered Bill. "We're a speedy pair. We can get you there."

It liked to tear along in a hurry, purring softly. It rushed down the street like a yellow streak with the two red lines blurred into one around its middle. It wiggled through the traffic.

Tom and his mother bounced and jounced on the leather seats. Tom's mother sat on the wide, soft one behind. But Tom sat on a little hard one so that he could look out of the window.

Then suddenly, squeak-jerk! The taxi stopped short. It stood stock still in the middle of the street. Ahead shone a bright red light. Underneath the light stood a big traffic policeman holding up his right hand.

Tom's mother called through the window, "Taxi driver-man, must you stop when lights are red? We simply have to get ahead. We're *terribly* late and the train won't wait."

And Bill answered, "Surely, lady, you have seen how cars must wait till lights are green. But we're a speedy pair, we'll surely get you there." Then suddenly, jerk-whizz! They were off again down the crowded street.

For the light had changed to green again.

Away went the taxi down the street faster than ever. Now it had to turn and twist, for the street was full of traffic—trucks and wagons and other taxis. The little taxi hurried past them all like a yellow streak and people could hardly see Tom's little face looking out of the window as he bounced and jounced by. "My!" said the people on the sidewalk.

"That's a speedy taxi. I wonder why it's in such a hurry. Lucky it's got such a good driver." The taxi wiggled around a big bus. It jiggled across a trolley track. Then suddenly, squeak-jerk! The little taxi stopped short again.

It stood stock still behind a big coal truck that was backing up to the sidewalk. For the driver was trying hard to get his truck just the right way for the black coal to go jumping and clattering down its slide into a hole in the sidewalk.

Tom stood up so that he could see the big coal truck better. He could see the handle on the side. He wished he could watch the driver turn that handle and make the big truck tip up in front. He wished they were not in such a hurry.

Tom's mother called through the window, "Taxi driver-man, first it's a cop that makes you stop and now we're stuck behind a truck. We're *awfully* late and the train won't wait."

So Bill called to the truck driver, "Please, will you try to let me get by?"

And the truck driver grinned and stopped his truck. Carefully and slowly Bill squeezed by the big coal truck, close to the sidewalk.

Bill called over his shoulder, "We're a speedy pair. We'll get you there."

Now the taxi went so fast that people skipped up onto the sidewalk as it went by and everyone thought: "That's the speediest taxi I ever saw!" Then suddenly, squeak-jerk! The taxi stopped short and Tom almost fell through the front window.

Tom's mother bounced so hard on the wide leather seat that her head whacked the ceiling of the taxi. Her hat slid down over one ear. Her big suitcase fell over with a bang on the floor and Tom's little suitcase hopped off the seat.

Tom's mother pulled her hat on straight again. Then she looked at her

watch. Then she looked out of the window at all the taxis and buses and trucks.

Once more she called to Bill on the front seat,

"Taxi driver-man, first it's a cop that makes you stop; then you get stuck behind a truck. Now the traffic is in our way. We're likely to sit here the rest of the day. We're *horribly* late and the train won't wait!"

So Bill began to blow his horn. "Honk! honk!" shrieked the little taxi. "Honk! honk! HONK!!!

"We want to go. You make us slow! We're a speedy pair. We want to get there.
*Honk!*

HONK!!!

# Honk!
# Honk!"

116

The nearer they came to the station, the more taxis and buses and trucks there were on the street.

Past them all the speedy taxi wiggled and jiggled, twisting and turning and curving and dodging. Tom jounced so hard on the little let-down seat that he could hardly see all the trucks and taxis and wagons and buses on the street.

Suddenly they stopped, and Bill blew the horn again.

"Honk!

Honk!

HONK!"

Tom's mother put her fingers in her ears. She thought, "Here we sit. We really need wings, to pass so many poky things."

But Tom shouted to the taxi driver-man in a loud voice to make him hear, "Do it again, please; do it again, please!"

And the taxi driver-man honked again.

Down the street, up above the station, they could see the big station clock. In five minutes the train would go. They really were very, terribly, awfully, horribly late, and they knew the train wouldn't wait.

Then suddenly, jerk, jerk! The traffic began to move. First a taxi, then a bus, then a truck, then more taxis, more buses, more trucks, till the whole line was moving. The speedy little taxi wiggled through the traffic. It dodged around a bus and it twisted around a truck and it whizzed past a taxi. Tom's mother kept looking at the big station clock. It said four minutes before the train went. Then three minutes. Then two minutes—and the little taxi drew up by the station.

Tom jumped out of the taxi while his mother gave Bill the money. She grabbed her big suitcase. Tom grabbed his little suitcase. And off they ran, thump, thump, thump, thumpety, thumpety, thumpety.

Bill looked after them and grinned at his yellow taxi. "Sure," he said. "We're a speedy pair—we got them there."

And it was true. The conductor was just ready to signal the engineer to start.

But he saw Tom and his mother come running down the platform and he waited for them. He took the big suitcase from Tom's mother, held the door open for her, and handed her the big suitcase. Tom stepped on the train after her, panting from his run and holding his little suitcase.

"All aboard!" called the conductor, waving his hand to the engineer.

Then the conductor swung onto the train. "You're a fast runner," he said to Tom. And to Tom's mother he said, "Lady, you just made it."

Tom was still breathing hard but he managed to gasp out, "We made it—because—we had such a speedy taxi—and speedy driver. You should have seen—that taxi hurry!"

# A YEAR IN THE CITY

## SPRING TIME

*Painters paint the railing red,*
*Tulips bloom in tulip bed,*
*Pushcart men with flowers shout,*
*Hurdy gurdies wheel about.*

By Lucy Sprague Mitchell

# SUMMER TIME

In the park the fountains play,
Children romp around all day,
Sprinkling carts come down the street
And cool the tired children's feet.

# FALL TIME

Leaves are falling, nights are cool,
Bigger children go to school,
Coal goes rattling down the chute,
Time for warmer dress or suit.

# WINTER TIME

Snow plows clear away the snow,
Autos skid unless they're slow,
The river's full of floating ice,
And Christmas trees on streets smell nice.

# THE MERRY SHIPWRECK

## By Georges Duplaix

LIFE was very peaceful on the barge. Every morning Captain Barnacle would look at the East River and cock his weather eye. He knew whether it would rain before night.

When it did rain, the crew huddled

around him while he spun a salty yarn about far-away places, shipwrecks, and oceans. Why, one would think the world was full of oceans!

"Hee-haw!" laughed the donkey, quite sure there was no such thing as a shipwreck. The kittens snuggled closer to their mother. But the ducklings could hardly wait to grow up and sail the seven seas!

On clear mornings, after Captain Barnacle had listened to all the Shipping News on the radio, he went off to market, and to chat with the crew's many friends ashore.

But one day, while Captain Barnacle was away, mother mouse crept into the galley. And while she ate a piece of cheese, her little mice were sharpening their teeth on the rope that held the barge fast to the pier.

Suddenly—before the parrot could

say, "Jack Robinson!"—the rope snapped, and the barge was heading down the river! What a lark! All the animals hung over the side to wave good-by to Captain Barnacle who was just coming back with his basket.

The cow steered, the donkey poled, and the pig waved a towel at all the tugs they passed.

They reached the end of the river, and traveling was such fun that no one noticed when the sun slipped under a cloud.

The sky grew dark. Soon there was thunder and lightning and wind and rain. Big waves slapped against the barge, rolling it this way and that.

The crew bellowed and barked and bleated and meowed for dear life.

Finally, after tossing the helpless barge

on a rock, the storm passed by. But there they were, shipwrecked and lost at sea, and very unhappy. Only the ducks didn't mind being soaking wet.

Many hours passed. At last they heard a boat whistle.

"Ship ahoy!" cried the parrot.

"Hurrah!" cried all the animals. "We're saved!"

Just then the sun came out again and they saw a red Fireboat, which was coming to their rescue.

"Come aboard!" cried the Fire Chief. And whom did they find on the boat but Captain Barnacle!

Soon they were scampering all over the Fireboat. The donkey aimed the hose at the sky, the goat paraded the

deck in fireman's hat and boots, and the hens roosted on top of the red funnel. Then it was time for dinner.

After dinner they went for a ride around the harbor, past ferryboats, tugs, tankers, yachts, battleships, rowboats, coal barges, liners, and freighters. But the Fireboat, looking like a red-and-gold Circus Boat, was far and away the finest of all.

At last everyone decided to have a look at the Statue of Liberty, and they sailed right up to it, landing on the little island underneath.

"Well, by cracky!" the keeper of the Statue of Liberty exclaimed. "Looks more like Noah's Ark than a Fireboat you've got there!"

On their way back they tied up alongside the battered barge. Poor Captain Barnacle looked very sad indeed.

"My poor barge!" he sobbed. "She was such a beautiful tub!"

"Never mind," said the Fire Chief. "Between your crew and mine we'll soon fix that!"

The firemen gave the animals lots of bright red paint, and a shiny brass bell

to hang over the galley door. And they all went to work.

When everything was finished, Captain Barnacle was pleased as punch. And so were the animals.

Then they thanked the firemen and clanged their new bell for a last good-by.

The animals were so happy to go home that they sang and shouted all the way up the East River. They made so

much noise that their friends heard them, and hurried down to the dock.

The butcher was there, and the grocer, and the junkman with his horse.

The window cleaner, the mailman, the delivery boy, and the Good Humor man were there. So was Tony the fruit man—along with all the boys and girls and alley cats in the neighborhood.

"It's good to be home!" said Captain Barnacle, shaking hands around. "Let's have a party!"

"Yes, let's!" everybody shouted. "Let's have a party! Hip, hip, hooray!"

They decorated the barge with Chinese lanterns, and Captain Barnacle cooked the best supper ever.

Just as he was ringing the bell, the firemen arrived and joined the party.

Before long, everyone was dancing around the deck, and singing songs in the moonlight.

# THE THREE BEARS

## *Told by Elsa Jane Werner*

ONCE upon a time there were three bears who lived in a little house in the woods. There was a great big father bear; there was a middle-sized mother bear; and there was a wee little baby bear.

One day the middle-sized mother bear had made a big batch of delicious porridge for dinner. She filled one great big bowl for the great big father bear, and one middle-sized bowl for herself, and a wee little bowl for the wee little baby bear. But it was still too hot to eat, so the three bears went for a little walk in the woods while they waited for their porridge to cool.

While the three bears were out in the woods, a little girl named Goldilocks came to the house. She knocked at the

door, but of course no one answered, since no one was at home. So Goldilocks opened the door, which was a rather naughty thing to do, and walked right in.

There she saw the three steaming bowls of porridge waiting on the table, and suddenly she was very hungry. So she picked up a spoon and sampled the porridge in the great big father bear's bowl.

"This is too hot," said Goldilocks.

So she tasted the porridge in the middle-sized mother bear's bowl.

"This is too cold," she said.

Then she tasted the wee little baby bear's porridge.

"This is just right," said Goldilocks, and she ate it all up.

Next she looked around for a place to sit. She tried the great big father bear's chair, but it was too hard. She tried the middle-sized mother bear's chair, but it was too soft. Then she tried the wee little baby bear's chair, and it was just right. But when she had been sitting in it for a few moments it broke all to pieces, and down went Goldilocks onto the floor.

Picking herself up, she climbed the stairs to the bedroom. First she tried the great big father bear's bed, but it was too high at the head for her. Then she tried the middle-sized mother bear's bed, but it was too high at the foot for her. At last she tried the wee little baby bear's bed, and it was so comfortable that she curled up on it and fell fast asleep.

By this time the three bears had decided that their porridge should be cool enough, so they came back from their walk in the woods.

No sooner had the great big father bear walked into the house than he let out a great big roar.

"Someone has been eating my porridge," he said in his great big voice.

"Someone has been eating my porridge," said the middle-sized mother bear in her middle-sized voice.

"Someone has been eating my porridge," said the wee little baby bear in his wee little voice, "and has eaten it all up!"

Puzzled, the three bears started to sit down to think things over. But the great big father bear let out another roar.

"Someone has been sitting in my chair," said the great big father bear in his great big voice.

The mother bear threw up her paws in surprise.

"Someone has been sitting in my chair," she said in her middle-sized voice.

At that the baby bear burst into tears.

"Someone has been sitting in my chair," he said in his wee little voice, "and has broken it all to pieces!"

The great big father bear took one look at the smashed pieces of the wee little chair and stamped off up the stairs, followed by the middle-sized mother bear and the wee little baby bear.

In the bedroom the great big father bear let out another great big roar.

"Someone has been mussing up my bed," he said in his great big voice.

The middle-sized mother bear hurried up to peer over his shoulder.

"Someone has been mussing up my bed," she said in her middle-sized voice.

The wee little baby bear pushed past them and ran over to his wee little bed.

"Someone has been mussing up my bed," he said in his wee little voice, "and here she is, asleep."

Sure enough, there was Goldilocks, still fast asleep. But the baby bear's shrill little voice woke her at last. Up she sat and rubbed her eyes, and at the sight of the three bears standing there she jumped out of bed, ran to the window, leaped down to the ground, and scampered away through the woods.

And never again did she wander near the three bears' house in the woods.

# SEVEN LITTLE POSTMEN

*By Margaret Wise Brown
and Edith Thacher Hurd*

A boy had a secret. It was a surprise.
He wanted to tell his grandmother.
So he sent his secret through the mail.

144

The story of that letter
Is the reason for this tale
Of the seven little postmen who carried the mail.
Because there was a secret in the letter,
The boy sealed it with red sealing wax.
If anyone broke the seal
The secret would be out.
He slipped the letter into the mail box.

The first little postman
Took it from the box,
Put it in his bag,
And walked seventeen blocks
To a big post office
All built of rocks.
The letter with the secret
Was dumped on a table
With big and small letters

That all needed the label
Of the big post office.
Stamp stamp,
Clickety click,
The machinery ran with
A quick sharp tick.
The letter with the secret is
Stamped at last,
And the round black circle tells
That it passed
Through the cancelling machine.
Click   whizz   fast!

Big letters,
Small letters,
Thin and tall—
The second little postman
Sorts them all.
The letters are sorted
From East to West,
From North to South.
"And this letter
Had best go West,"
Said the second
Little postman,
Scratching his chest.
Into the pouch,
Lock it tight—

148

The secret letter
Must travel all night.
The third little postman in the big mail car
Comes to a crossroad where waiting are
A green, a yellow, and a purple car.
They all stop there. There is nothing to say.
The mail truck has the right of way!
"The mail must go through!"
Up and away through sleet and hail
This airplane carries the fastest mail.

The pilot flies through whirling snow
As far and as fast as the plane can go.
And he drops the mail for the evening train.
Now hang the pouch on the big hook crane!
The engine speeds up the shining rails
And the fourth little postman
Grabs the mail with a giant hook.

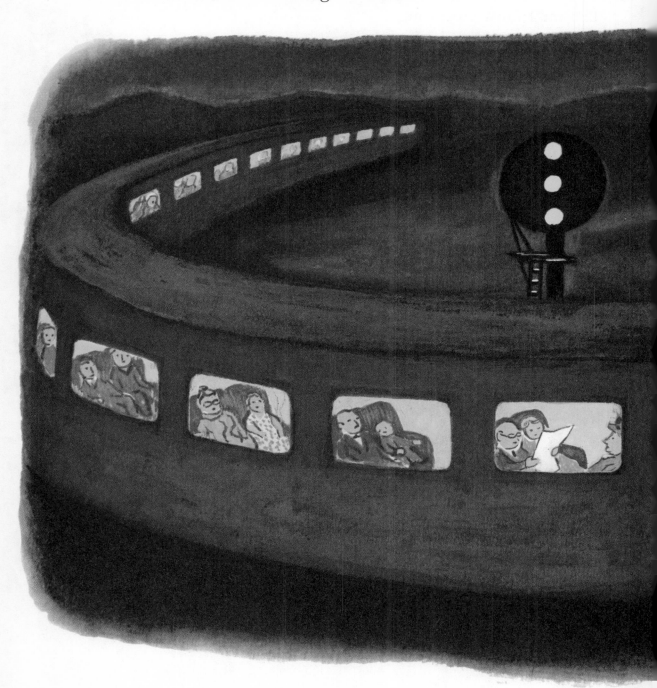

The train roars on
With a puff and a snort
And the fourth little postman
Begins to sort.
The train carries the letter
Through gloom of night
In a mail car filled with electric light

To a country postman
By a country road
Where the fifth little postman
Is waiting for his load.

The mail clerk
Heaves the mail pouch
With all his might
To the fifth little postman
Who grabs it tight.

Then off he goes
Along the lane
And over the hill
Until
He comes to a little town
That is very small—
So very small
The post office there
Is hardly one at all.

The sixth little postman
In great big boots
Sorts the letters
For their various routes—
Some down the river,
Some over the hill.
But the secret letter
Goes farther still.
The seventh little postman
On R.F.D.
Carries letters and papers,
Chickens and fruit
To the people who live
Along his route.

He stops to deliver some sugar
To Mr. Jones who keeps a store
And always seems
To need something more.
For Mrs. O'Finnigan
With all her ills
He brings a bottle
Of bright pink pills.
And an airmail letter
That cost eight cents
He hands to a farmer
Over the fence.

There was a Special Delivery.
Sign for it here.
Sign your name,
And write it clear.

There were parts
For a tractor
And a wig for an actor

And a funny post card
For a little boy
Playing in his own backyard.

There was something for Sally
And something for Sam

And something for Mrs. Potter
Who was busy making jam.

There were dozens of chickens
For Mrs. Pickens

And a dress for a party
For Mrs. McCarty.

At the last house along the way sat the grandmother of the boy who had sent the letter with the secret in it. She had been wishing all day he would come to visit. For she lived all alone in a tiny house and sometimes felt quite lonely.

The postman blew his whistle and gave her the letter with the red sealing wax on it—the secret letter!

"Sakes alive! What is it about?"
Sakes alive! The secret is out!
What does it say?

DEAREST GRANNY:
I AM WRITING TO SAY
THAT I'M COMING TO VISIT ON SATURDAY.
MY CAT HAS SEVEN KITTENS AND I AM BRINGING
ONE TO YOU FOR YOUR VERY OWN KITTEN.
THE POSTMAN IS MY FRIEND.
YOUR GRANDSON
THOMAS

ONE morning, a very small puppy woke up in a brand-new doghouse.

He sniffed at the cozy, dark inside . . . and he licked at the bright blue outside.

Then he blinked his eyes and looked all around the big busy barnyard.

"It's a wonderful place," he said to himself, "but oh, my, isn't it big?"

Just as he said that, all the big barnyard animals came running up to him.

"Are you the new watchdog?" asked the ducks. The little puppy liked that

# LITTLE YIP-YIP AND HIS BARK

*By Kathryn and Byron Jackson*

160

watchdog idea. He smiled and wagged his tail.

"I guess I am!" he said.

"Well then," crowed the big rooster, "let's hear your big watchdog bark!"

The puppy stood up tall and opened his mouth.

He took a deep breath.

And he barked, "Yip-yip-yip!"

The rooster turned to the pigs. "Did you hear anything?" he asked.

"We heard *something*," squealed the pigs. "It sounded like a squeaky shoe!"

And the calf said she thought it sounded like a baby robin calling its mother.

All the animals laughed and ran away very busily, and the puppy went into his new house.

"Maybe my barking isn't all it should be," he said, and he ran out in the sunshine to practice.

But before he had time for one yip, a great big black dog came bounding up.

That big dog tasted the puppy's milk, and he nibbled the puppy's biscuit.

"Puppy food!" he snorted. "I'll come

161

back when you have some real food for me to eat up!"

And he walked away with his head in the air.

The little puppy felt so cross that he barked until that big dog was out of sight.

"Yip-yip-yip!" he barked.

A little field mouse, on its way to the corn crib, heard that little bark. It jumped when it heard the first yip, but when it heard the second and third it sat down and laughed until the tears dripped off its whiskers.

"Oh, ho, ho!" laughed the mouse. "I have baby mice at home who can bark louder than that!"

"Is that so!" cried the puppy. He ran at the mouse with all his sharp little teeth showing.

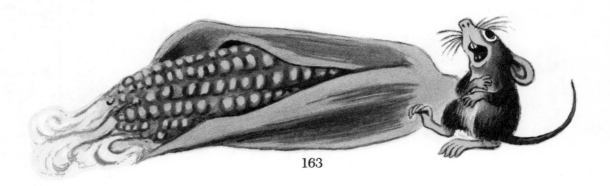

163

"I'll bite you into three pieces!" he barked, and he chased the mouse across the barnyard.

But the mouse was gone! It had disappeared through the cracks in the corn crib, and the puppy was chasing nobody at all.

"Well," he barked proudly, "I guess I scared *him* all right!"

And then he heard all the mice in the corn crib barking little tiny barks.

"Yip-yip-yip," they laughed. "Yip-yip! Oh, what a watchdog!"

He looked for something bigger to scare.

And just as it was getting dark he saw something *much* bigger.

A slim, sly, red fox came creeping into the barnyard.

He slithered straight toward the hen house, and he looked so mean and hungry that the little puppy backed away from him.

"I'll have to bark louder than ever this time," he whispered bravely, and he backed right into an empty milk pail. "You have to bark very loud to scare a fox."

The sly fox crept nearer and nearer and nearer to the hen house, licking his chops and snickering to himself. And then, all at once, the puppy took a deep breath and barked.

When that little bark came out of the milk pail, it wasn't a little yip-yip-yip at all! It echoed and rumbled around in

the pail, and when it came out, it was a fine big bark.

It went: BOW-WOW-WOW! and it was so loud that the puppy jumped in the air, pail and all.

"Help!" squeaked the fox. He turned head over heels, and away he ran as fast as he could go.

The puppy picked himself up and barked a little yip-yip.

He ran back into the pail and barked a big BOW-WOW.

"Now I know how to scare the wits

"Rabbits in the cabbage patch!" the rooster crowed. "Spoiling the whole cabbage patch!"

The little puppy woke up with a start. He ran across the barnyard and into the garden, barking his little yip-yip-yip.

And the rabbits stopped eating just long enough to swallow what they had in their mouths.

Then they jumped up and down on a row of young cabbages, laughing at that sleepy little bark.

"Oh, bad!" yipped the puppy. He started toward his milk pail. And then he said, "Oh, good!" and scampered into an empty barrel that was lying at the edge of the cabbage patch.

"Now for my best rabbit-scaring bark!" thought the little puppy. He closed his

out of anything!" he cried. "All I have to do is hide in an empty something before I bark!"

And he trotted back to his brand-new house with his little tail wagging so fast that it looked like a pinwheel.

Next morning, a family of hungry rabbits hopped into the farm garden.

They chewed tunnels in the biggest cabbages, and hopped through the tunnels. They bit big holes in the middle-sized cabbages, and little holes in the tiny little cabbages.

one second there wasn't a rabbit to be seen!

"That was even better than the milk pail!" laughed the little puppy.

Then he thought he might find something still louder. He nosed all around the farm, barking in every empty thing he found.

He barked in a rusty milk can.

And he barked in a big round pipe.

And then one day he found an old oil drum.

He ran in that and barked, "Where's that big black dog now?"

And it sounded like this:

**BOW WOW WOW WOW WOW WOW !!**

eyes and puffed out his chest and barked as loudly as he could.

The big, echoey barrel rolled the sound out, big and loud, into the garden.

It came out such a big BOW-WOW-WOW that the rabbits' ears stood on end.

"Watchdogs!" they cried. "At least four great big ones!"

They hopped lickety-split out of the cabbage patch and over the fence. In

The puppy liked that oil-drum bark. He practiced it every day—and every day his own little bark grew bigger and bigger. But he never noticed that.

The farmer didn't like all this noise.

"You're a fine watchdog, little puppy," he said. "But you'll have to use your own little bark after tomorrow, because I'm going to clean up the farm."

The next day while the farmer worked, the puppy ran at his heels.

"Oh, don't take my barrel!" he barked.

And he barked, "Don't take my oil-drum!"

And then he barked, "Don't take my milk can—or that old pipe. Oh, I need those old pails!"

But into the junk wagon they went.

"All my barking things are gone," cried the little puppy. "Now, what will I do when that big black dog comes back?"

And the very minute he said that, along came the big black dog! He walked boldly through the puppy's barnyard.

He walked right up to the little puppy's house.

He licked up all the puppy's milk, and then he picked up the puppy's new chewing bone.

That was too much for the little puppy.

He ran at the big black dog like a small thunderbolt.

He was so angry that he barked for all he was worth, and by this time his own bark was a real big

## BOW WOW WOW!

It was even bigger than his oil-drum bark!

The big dog never stopped to see how big the little puppy was. He just dropped that bone and ran, with the puppy snapping at his tail. He jumped over the fence, he raced down the road, and he *never* came back.

Everybody on the farm came running out to see that chase.

"Just look at our watchdog!" squealed the pigs.

169

"And just listen to his bark!" the rooster crowed.

The farmer's wife was so pleased that she ran into the house for an old soft pillow. She put it in the doghouse.

"It will make a nice bed for our watchdog," she said.

The farmer filled the puppy's bowl with cream. He brought out a little dish of gravy with some fine juicy scraps of meat in it. He put a new chewing bone full of tid-bits beside the old chewing bone. And then he whistled a long, loud whistle for the little puppy.

When the little puppy got back to his house, he was the most surprised puppy in the whole world.

First, he barked a good-sized bark to

say "Thank you," and then he began to eat. He ate until his little sides were as round as a pumpkin.

He tried out his lovely new bed.

It was so soft and comfortable that he almost fell asleep.

But he had one more thing to do.

The little puppy stood up on his four little feet and wagged his tail.

And just to make sure he was really a real watchdog, at last, he barked the loudest kind of bark—

BOW WOW WOW

# FIRE ENGINES

Ding, ding, ding! goes the alarm.
The firemen slide down the pole.

Ding, ding, ding! goes the fire-engine bell.

The Chief is on his way.

Clang, clang, clang!

Through the streets goes the hose car.

Here comes the hook and ladder!

The people come running to see.

Hurry, hurry! Connect the hoses!
S-s-s-s! goes the water.

Crank, crank. Up go the ladders.
Up go the firemen with the hoses.

Chop, chop, chop! go the axes.
Crash! go the windows.

Down the ladders. Into the net.
Save things from the fire!

Sput, sput, sput! Out goes the fire.

Firemen and people go home.

# HOUSES
## By Elsa Jane Werner

Houses, houses, houses! Everyone lives in some kind of a house. Don't you? Maybe it is a small house on a quiet street.

Maybe it is a big apartment house where a lot of families live. Maybe it is a middle-sized house in a nice middle-sized town. Maybe it is a trailer in a

trailer park. But everyone lives in some kind of a house. Because everyone needs a home.

"Why do people need houses?" you ask. Well, a house keeps you dry when it rains. Some places it rains almost every day. There the houses may stand high up on stilts.

Or they may be built in trees. Tree houses have steep roofs so the rain slides down, and the home inside stays dry.

A house keeps you warm in the cold. In some places there is snow much of the year. Even the houses may be built of cakes of snow.

These houses are called igloos.

In other lands, houses may be built of mud.

A house shelters you from the wind. It may be a warm round house of felt, with no corners for the wind to whistle past. It may be a chalet with stones on the roof, to keep the wind from blowing it away.

A house shelters you from the sun. It may be a tent to keep you in the shade, or a house with thick, cool walls. It may be a woven hut of brush—or of grass. But if you live there, it is home.

Yes, wherever you live you need a house. But what will you build it of?

If you live in a land with lots of trees, you may build your house of wood. It may be a cabin of round brown logs, or a white-painted Colonial house.

It may be half-timbered, with a steep, gabled roof, or even a wooden gypsy cart.

If you live in a land with no tall trees, you may build your house of clay. You may use bricks shaped smooth and burned hard. You may have a house of bricks.

You may use thick adobe blocks of clay and straw dried in the sun. And you'll wash the adobe walls with color. You will have a nice adobe house.

You may build your house of the stone around you. Some people's houses are partly caves. Some live up on the tops of cliffs, where no one can take them by surprise.

Some houses of stone are castles—very old, with towers from which to watch the countryside.

You may build your house of solid stone. You may build it lightly of delicate woods, with some walls of paper the light comes through. If the earth should tremble and the house fall down, you could quickly build it up again.

Your house may be a boat on a river or a sea.

You may have steel girders inside your walls, so you can build a house that is very tall. You may squeeze your house in, tight, between two others that are just as tall.

Or you may set it down in the middle of a lawn, with space for children to play.

Yes, everybody needs a house and home. Which kind will you choose?

# THE HAPPY MAN
# AND HIS DUMP TRUCK

*By Miryam*

Once upon a time there was a man who had a dump truck. Every time he saw a friend, he would wave his hand and tip the dumper.

One day he was riding in his dump truck, singing a happy song, when he met a pig going along the road.

"Would you like a ride in my dump truck?" he asked.

"Oh, thank you!" said the pig. And he climbed into the back of the truck.

After they had gone a little way down the road, the man saw a friend. He waved his hand and tipped the dumper.

"Whee," said the pig. "What fun!"
And he slid all the way down to the
bottom of the dumper.

Very soon they came to a farm.

"Here is where my friends live," said
the pig. "You have a nice dump truck.

"Would you please let my friends see your truck?"

"I will give them a ride in my dump truck," said the man.

199

So the hen and the rooster climbed into the truck. And the duck climbed into the truck. And the dog and the cat climbed into the truck. And the pig climbed back into the truck, too. And the man closed the tail gate, so they would not fall out.

And then off they went!

They went past the farm, and all the animals waved to the farmer. The man was very happy. "They are all my friends," he said. So he waved his hand, and tipped the dumper.

The hen, the rooster, the duck, the dog, the cat, and the pig all slid down the dumper into a big heap!

The hen clucked.

The duck quacked.

The rooster crowed.

202

The dog barked.

The cat mewed.

And the pig said a great big grunt.

The animals were all so happy! Then the man took them for a long ride, and drove them back to the farm.

He opened the tail gate wide and raised the dumper all the way up. All the animals slid off the truck onto the ground.

"What a fine sliding-board," they all said.

"Thank you," said all the animals.

"Cut, cut," clucked the hen. "Cock-a-doodle-doo," the rooster crowed. "Quack, quack," quacked the duck. "Bow-wow," barked the dog. "Meow, meow," mewed the cat.

And the pig said a great big grunt. "Oink, oink!"

The man waved his hand and tipped the dumper, and he rode off in his dump truck, singing a happy song.

# LION CUB'S BUSY DAY

## By Barbara Shook Hazen

It was nap time in the jungle.
Lion Cub's father was sound asleep
and snoring. So were his brother
and sister.

"You too, Lion Cub," said his mother.
"You need a nap. I can tell."

But the minute she wasn't watching,
Lion Cub sneaked through the tall grass.

He wasn't a bit sleepy.
He felt like playing.

"Will you play with me?"
Lion Cub asked a leopard
stretched out on a tree branch.

The leopard was in the middle
of an enormous yawn.

"Not today," she said.
"I'm terribly tired.
Maybe tomorrow."

Lion Cub scampered on. He came to an elephant tugging at a tree.

"Please play with me," said Lion Cub.

Lion Cub liked elephants. They were fun to ride and their trunks made wonderful swings.

But this elephant was busy.
He didn't even bother to answer.

The elephant gave a mighty yank.
The tree uprooted, and Lion Cub
got out of the way just in time.

Next Lion Cub saw
five monkeys in a tree.
One was eating a banana.
Another was scratching
his brother's back, and two
were swinging in the branches.

"They look very busy," said Lion Cub.

He walked on.

Suddenly he tripped over something. The something looked like the tapered tip of a fat, spotted rope.

What could it be and where did it lead?

Lion Cub wanted to find out.

He followed the coils and curves of the something till he came to the other end, which turned out to be the head of a python.

The python had been asleep in the sun. He was just waking up.

"Will you play with me?" asked Lion Cub.

"Come closer," said the python. "I like lion cubs, especially plump young ones."

Lion Cub came a little closer.

But those cold glistening coils didn't look a bit inviting.

"No, thank you," he said.

Lion Cub still felt like
playing with someone.
So he walked down to
the river bank.

There he saw three hippopotamuses
playing water games.

They were gurgling and grunting
and having a rollicking good time.

"Come out and play with me,"
pleaded Lion Cub.

"You come out and join us,"
said one of the hippos.

But Lion Cub didn't want
to get his feet wet.

"I'll come out and play with you."
said a sly crocodile.

He opened his great cave of a mouth.

Lion Cub didn't hesitate a second longer.
He turned and ran through the tall swamp grass.
All the crocodile could see was a tassel of tail.

Lion Cub ran till he came to
a couple of friendly giraffes.

"Will you play with me—oh, please?"
Lion Cub asked.

"We would but you're too far from us,"
said the giraffes.

Some zebras raced by
and fled in a cloud of dust.

"I guess they don't like lions,
even little ones," said Lion Cub sadly.

Then Lion Cub saw that the zebras
were not running from him.

A bad-tempered rhinoceros was charging after the zebras.
He snorted, stamped his feet, and crashed blindly into a tree.
The eyesight of the rhinoceros was as terrible as his temper.
The poor beast could hardly see.

Lion Cub crouched behind a bush
till he was gone.

Suddenly Lion Cub felt sad and
out of sorts himself.

He found a soft, leafy place to sit
and he started to cry.

"Nobody wants to play with me,"
he sobbed.

"I want to play with you," said Lion Cub's large tawny mother, who had been following behind and watching a long while.

"But first," she said sternly, "you are going to take a good long nap. All cubs, even little lions, need their rest. And you were naughty to run away. I am very angry with you."

His mother lifted Lion Cub by the scruff of his neck.

She wouldn't stay angry long. Lion Cub knew that. And it was nice to feel cozy and cared for. Later there would be plenty of time to play.

Gently, his mother laid Lion Cub down. "Close your sleepy eyes," she purred.

And all at once Lion Cub did feel sleepy, after all. It had been a busy day, for a Lion Cub.

# THE SEVEN SNEEZES

*By Olga Cabral*

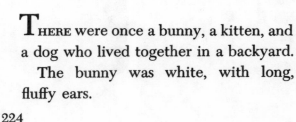

THERE were once a bunny, a kitten, and a dog who lived together in a backyard. The bunny was white, with long, fluffy ears.

224

The kitten was black, and like all kittens it had teeny ears.

The dog was a great big dog with a great big bark.

Everybody was happy, everybody was satisfied. The bunny loved his big ears, the kitten was glad that her ears were tiny, and the dog was proud of his great big bark.

One day a rag man came along in an old wagon.

"Any rags today? Any rags today?" sang the rag man.

It was a chilly day. The rag man started to sneeze—

"Any r-ah-ah-ah-ah-"

The bunny, the kitten, and the dog all held their breath until the rag man finished his sneeze—

"A-choo! A-cha! A-chachoo!"

They were three hearty sneezes. So hearty, that the rag man was blown out of sight down the road—wagon and horse and all!

"Goodness gracious—" the bunny, the kitten, and the dog started to say to each other. And then they saw something strange had happened to them!

The black kitten had the bunny's long, white ears.

The white bunny had the kitten's teeny, black ears.

227

"Why, how silly you both look!" said the dog.

The next minute, he felt silly. Because, when he opened his mouth no big bark came out, only a teeny little meow.

Things were certainly mixed up!

The bunny felt his short, teeny ears. He squeaked.

The kitten felt her long, overgrown ears.

"Goodness gracious me!" she said.

But she said it in a terrible, great big bark! And she fell over backward, so surprised was she to hear herself barking.

Then the kitten saw her teeny ears on the bunny's head. "Give me back my ears!" she said.

She ran over to the bunny and tried to pull them off.

The bunny saw his long ears on the kitten's head.

"Give me back my ears!" he said.

He tried to pull them off too.

And the dog ran around and around them, meowing like a cat.

"Oh, dear!" barked the cat. "This will never do. What do you think happened to us?"

"Everything was fine," meowed the dog, "until the rag man came."

The bunny had hiccups, he was so upset.

"The—sneezes—did—it!" he said between hiccups.

They brought him a drink of water.

"Oh, dear!" barked the cat. "That's just what happened! Those awful sneezes mixed everything up!"

"Now what are we going to do?" said the dog in his baby-kitten voice.

They thought and thought and then the bunny said,

"We must find the rag man."

"That's it!" said the kitten. "We will show him what his sneezes did!"

"And make him put everything back the way it was," said the dog. "If he can!"

So they set out to find the rag man.

They went along and soon they met a goose without any feathers. She was carrying all her feathers in a little basket.

"Pardon us," said the bunny, the cat, and the dog, "but did you see a rag man go by this way?"

"Can't you see that he did?" asked the goose, angrily stamping her foot. "He sneezed off all my feathers! And I'm going to find him and make him put them back on again—if he can!"

So they all went along together.

Pretty soon they met a rooster carrying his comb in his beak. He looked very queer because his tail feathers grew on top of his head.

"Pardon us," said the bunny, the cat, the dog, and the pink goose, "but did you see—"

229

"Don't say another word!" said the rooster angrily, dropping his comb and picking it up again. "That awful rag man! It's wicked to go around sneezing folks into trouble, that way! My lovely red comb! In the dust! I'm going to make him put it back again—if he can!"

So they all went along together.

Pretty soon they met a little boy. He was sitting on a fence, rubbing his eyes.

He looked very queer because he was wearing only half a jacket, and only one shoe. He was holding the other half of his jacket. And the other shoe was upside down on top of his head. It looked like a strange kind of cap.

"Pardon us—" began the bunny, the cat, the dog, the goose, and the rooster.

The little boy stopped rubbing his eyes. He saw all the funny animals. He heard the cat bark and the dog meow. He laughed and laughed and laughed until he fell right off the fence. And then he went right on laughing.

"So you've been sneezed at too?" the little boy said to the funny animals. "Well, don't feel bad. Don't you see what a fix I'm in? Just look at my nice new jacket. And my shoe on top of my head. It's sneezed on so tight it won't come off. I've pulled and I've pulled."

He pulled again to show them. They each pulled. No, the shoe wouldn't come off the little boy's head. It was sneezed on for good.

"Let's find that rag man," he said, "and make him take it off—if he can!"

So they all went along together.

And pretty soon they met a little girl standing in the road, curling her toes and crying. She held two long braids in her hand, the color of taffy candy. They were very pretty pigtails. Each was tied with a beautiful ribbon.

What a pity they had been sneezed right off her head!

The animals were all very sorry. So was the little boy. But there was nothing they could do. The pigtails could not be stuck on again.

But when the little girl saw what a fix everyone else was in she giggled. She dried her tears. And they all went along together to look for the rag man.

They walked and they walked. And by and by they came to a tumble-down house with a tumble-down fence around it. An old horse and an old wagon stood in front of the house. And somebody inside was getting ready to sneeze—

*"Ah-ah-ah-ah-ah-"*

They all held their breath and waited for the sneeze to come. It came—

*"Kerchaya!"*

The sneeze blew the horse and wagon up into the air. They came down again on the roof of the tumble-down house.

"This is the right place, all right!" said the little boy.

And they all ran up and knocked on the door.

The rag man came to the door wiping his eyes.

"Why, come in, my dears!" he said to the little boy and the little girl. "Come in, my pets!" he said to the animals.

They all went inside and sat down in the kitchen.

The rag man wiped the tears out of his eyes. And now he really saw them.

"Oh-ho-ho-ho!" he laughed. "Oh-ho-ho-ho-ho!"

"What are you laughing at?" barked the cat.

"You did it, with your awful sneezes!" meowed the dog.

"Oh-ho-ho-ho-ho-ho!" laughed the rag man. He wiped his eyes again. He blew his nose.

"So—that's—how I—sneeze!"

Everyone was angry as could be because the rag man laughed at what he had done. They all jumped up and crowded around him.

"What will my mother say when I tell her I've lost my pigtails?" cried the little girl.

"They'll laugh at me in school with a shoe on my head!" cried the little boy.

"No one will love me with these little ears!" squeaked the bunny.

"Or me with these big ears!" barked the cat.

"How can I guard the house without my great big bark?" meowed the dog.

"I'll freeze without my feathers!" cried the goose.

"No barnyard will have me!" cried the rooster.

"Now, now, now," said the rag man, trying to calm everybody. "Don't be angry, my dears. Don't be angry, my pets. Indeed, I had no idea how much damage my sneezes could do. I don't quite understand myself how it happened. Let me think a minute."

They all sat down again to let the rag man think.

By

and by

he said,

"I think it's because I sometimes sneeze magic words. A funny word comes out, and some kind of magic happens. But I never know what it's going to be, because I never sneeze the same way twice in a row."

"Well, what are you going to do about us?" all the visitors asked.

"I'll try and sneeze everything right again," said the rag man. "But what that magic word may be, I have no idea. So I'll just have to keep sneezing and sneezing, until the right word comes out!"

They all waited for the rag man to begin sneezing.

"I don't feel very sneezy just now," he said after a while. He pointed to a

shelf where a can of pepper stood. "Just sprinkle some on my nose," he begged. "It will help me get started."

The little girl did what the rag man asked. The rag man sneezed—just an ordinary, everyday sneeze:

*"Splish."*

Just like that.

And nothing happened. Nothing at all.

"I'll have to sneeze harder," said the rag man. "More pepper, please—lots more!"

The little girl took off the lid of the pepper can. And she poured a big swish of pepper on the rag man's nose.

And the rag man went—

234

*"Aah-huh-huh-huh-huh-huh-huh-"*

The little girl jumped back. They all held their breaths because they could see something was going to happen.

*"Choo! Buttonmyshoe! Switcheroo!"* The rag man finished sneezing.

Something happened, all right, but not what they all wanted.

The furniture flew out of the window! The house lifted into the air! So did the horse and wagon. So did the fence. And they all came down with a bang! In an utterly different place, a much nicer place than before.

They all got up and felt themselves. But nobody was hurt a bit.

"M-m-m-m-m-m-m-m-more—" the rag man gasped.

The little girl came forward. And she threw the whole can of pepper at the rag man!

The rag man opened his eyes—WIDE! And he opened his mouth—WIDE!

And seven big earthquake sneezes came out!

*"Katchoo!"*

The bunny's ears and the kitten's ears flew into the air! They came down again in their right places—the long, white ears on the bunny, and the teeny, black ears on the kitten!

*"Katchim!"*

The dog jumped into the air and barked!

*"Katcham!"*

The kitten mewed as she ran round and round the room!

*"Katchibble!"*

All the feathers flew out of the little basket and stuck onto the goose again!

*"Fumadiddle!"*

The rooster's comb flew onto his head and his tail feathers stuck where tail feathers should grow!

*"Skedaddle!"*

The little boy's jacket was sneezed

whole, and his shoe was sneezed back on his foot!

*"Fiddle-Faddle!"*

The little girl's pigtails flew back on her head and stuck there!

Everything was back the way it was!

"Dear me," said the rag man, wiping his eyes. "That was awfully hard work. But I'm glad everything is fixed again." All of a sudden he looked sneezy.

"Run!" cried the rag man. "Run, everybody, while I hold my nose!"

Everybody jumped up and ran out of the house
before
      the rag man
          could sneeze
              again!

And they ran and they ran all the way home!

# RUPERT
# THE RHINOCEROS

*By Carl Memling*

no matter who came near, Rupert always charged!

He charged at the timid kudu.

He charged at the spotted leopard.

IN a dense thicket in Deepest Africa there lived a rhinoceros.

His name was Rupert.

Rupert was really very nice. But everyone thought he was horrid, because . . .

239

He charged at the tall giraffe.

He even charged at the enormous elephant.

One day he charged at a hunter, but the hunter did not run away.

Suddenly the ground gave way under Rupert and he fell into a trap the hunter had made.

The hunter's helpers put him in a cage and took him to the port where their ship was anchored.

As the cage went up, Rupert said farewell to Deepest Africa.

One day, there was a terrible storm at sea.

Down in the hold of the pitching ship, Rupert's cage fell over with a *crash*—and the door sprang open!

Now Rupert was free!

But just as he climbed up on deck, a sailor came near. Rupert could not help himself; he charged again.

The sailor leaped aside —and Rupert crashed through the railing.

Luckily, a whale happened to swim by.

243

Rupert held on tight, and had a nice ride on the whale's back. After a long swim, the whale let him off near a beach, and Rupert said good-by

Behind the beach, Rupert found a city. By the light of the moon, he walked along the quiet streets, until at last he found a park and fell asleep.

In the morning, a parade came near the park.

People watched and people marched. The mayor rode in a long, long car. The drummers went BABBOOM, BAB-BOOM, BABBOOM—and Rupert woke up.

Rupert charged wildly again.

He charged at the people watching. He charged at the people marching. He charged at the drummers. He even charged at the mayor's long, long car.

Next day Rupert woke up in a hospital.

His horn was bandaged, and a kindly old doctor was taking his pulse.

"Don't worry, Rupert," said the doctor. "You'll be better soon."

Then the kindly doctor gave him an Eye Test. Rupert tried his best to read the Eye Chart. But all that he could see was a fuzzy blur.

"Hmmm," said the doctor. "Just as I thought, Rupert. You are really very nice, but . . .

" . . . you have very poor eyesight. No matter who comes near, *you* see only a

fuzzy blur. That frightens you—and that is why you're always charging wildly."

The doctor opened a large white drawer.

And he fitted Rupert with a pair of glasses.

As they both walked out, Rupert cried happily, "How clear everything looks now! I'll never charge at anyone again!"

But, at the sight of Rupert, people scrambled into doorways and hid behind trees.

245

"Dear me," said the doctor. "They're still afraid of you. But don't cry, Rupert. They'll know better soon."

The doctor phoned his friends and said,

"Drop what you're doing, and come this instant! Don't change your clothes— come just as you are! We're going to have a party!"

The mayor dropped a fountain pen and came in his top hat.

The carpenter dropped a keg of nails and came in his apron.

The teacher dropped a piece of chalk and came in her teacher's smock.

The mechanic dropped a monkey wrench and came in his overalls.

Soon the doctor's house was filled with friends. They had all come just-as-they-were.

Then in came Rupert, wearing his glasses and a shy smile, and looking so

nice that even the littlest girl at the party was not afraid of him.

She gave him a garland of roses to show how much she liked him.

And now Rupert, like all RhinoceROSES had roses at
THE END.

# MAKE WAY FOR THE THRUWAY

## By Caroline Emerson

THE new thruway was being built. Men and machines worked week after week and month after month.

Rocks and trees had to be pushed aside. Hills had to be cut through. The new thruway would go the shortest, quickest way.

"Cars are in a hurry," said the Big Boss.

First came the bulldozer. Mike ran

the bulldozer. He was proud of his big machine. He called it Johnny.

"Anything that can be pushed," said Mike proudly, "we will push."

He steered Johnny toward a big rock. That rock had lain there for many, many years. Now the bulldozer began to push it slowly aside.

Under that rock a mother fox had her den. Her four baby foxes lay close beside her.

Slowly the big rock began to move.

What was happening? Was the world coming to an end? The mother fox dared not wait to see.

"Follow me!" she cried. Mother Fox and her four babies dashed off toward the woods.

Next Mike turned his bulldozer toward a clump of bushes. "We'll clear this next," he said to Johnny.

A cottontail rabbit had his home in those bushes. His little white tail shook with fear when he saw the great machine coming nearer and nearer.

Away dashed the little rabbit.

249

Then Mike steered the bulldozer toward a tall elm tree. The tree had grown on that spot for a hundred years. But now it must go.

Away flew a pair of robins whose nest was in the tree. They flew off into the woods to find a new home.

"Sorry," called Mike, "but the thruway must go through."

Down came the big elm tree with a crash.

Behind Mike's bulldozer came a back hoe to scoop up dirt.

Then came a crane. Tony ran the crane. He pulled a lever. Down swung the two big steel jaws.

They opened wide over some rocks, and lifted them slowly into the air. Tony swung the crane over and laid the rocks carefully in the dump truck.

"Anything that can be lifted," said Tony, "we'll lift."

Pedro drove the dump truck. He was a good driver.

Pedro backed a load of dirt and stone up to the very edge of a steep bank. Then up, up, up went the back of the truck. Crash! Bang! went the stones, to fill up the hollow.

There was a grader. It smoothed out the road.

There was a roller. It pressed down the earth.

There were trucks that poured crushed stone on the roadway.

"Anything that can be dumped," said Pedro, "we will dump."

After the rocks and dirt were cleared away, other machines came in.

Then came the spreaders. They spread on the concrete top.

Mike and Tony kept well ahead of the other machines.

"They do the easy work," said Mike to Tony. "We break ground. We're the earth movers."

One day Mike stopped his bulldozer and stared. Right in the middle of the new thruway stood a little old house. Tall trees grew over it. A yellow rose bush climbed over the front door.

"Well," said Mike, "I suppose we'll have to take that house down." Mike's bulldozer could knock a house down in half an hour.

Just then the door of the house opened. A little old lady stepped out. She shook her apron at some chickens scratching near the door. "Shoo!" she said.

Then she saw the big machines.

She shook her apron at them. "Shoo!" she said.

Mike climbed down from his bulldozer.

"I'm sorry, ma'am," he said politely, "but we have to take this house down."

"No, you haven't," said the little old lady.

"But the new thruway goes right through here," said Mike.

"No, it doesn't," said the little old lady.

"You'll be paid for your land," said Mike.

"Money isn't everything in this world," said the little old lady.

Mike scratched his head. "I'll have to ask the Big Boss," he said.

Mike climbed into his bulldozer and drove away.

Next day, the Big Boss drove to the little old house. "I'm sorry, ma'am," he said, "this house must come down."

"Young man," said the little old lady, "I've lived in this house for seventy years. I watched those trees grow. I planted that rose bush. I'm not leaving."

"But the thruway must go through," said the Big Boss. "People want the quickest, shortest way these days."

"What's their hurry?" asked the little old lady.

The Big Boss shook his head. He didn't know.

The little old lady looked at her rose bush. Then she turned to Mike.

"Does *your* mother grow roses?" she asked.

"Red roses grow all over her cottage," said Mike. "You can smell them as you come down the road."

"Does *your* mother grow roses?" she asked Tony.

"You never saw prettier ones!" said Tony proudly.

"The sweetest roses in the world are in Puerto Rico," said Pedro. "They grow in my mother's garden."

The little old lady looked at her yellow rose bush. "You see," she said to the Big Boss, "those machines can tear things down, but they can't grow roses like my roses."

Then she turned to Mike and Tony. "Take those machines away," she said. "Shoo!"

"I'll have to ask the Bigger Boss," said the Big Boss, and he drove off.

Mike and Tony and Pedro stood looking at the little old house. Then Mike turned to Tony.

"You know," Mike said slowly, "there's a low place over there. The road *could* run a little to the right."

"People driving by would like to see the roses," added Pedro.

Tony nodded. "There'll be a moon tonight," he said. "We could work late."

And they did. They worked all night in their big machines.

Next morning, back came the Big Boss with the Bigger Boss.

"Here's the house," said the Big Boss. "It's right in the middle of the new thruway—" And then he stopped.

There ahead lay the new roadway. The land had been cleared. The roadbed had been dug. The dirt had been smoothed.

The new road ran well to the right of the little old house.

"What's all this fuss about?" shouted the Bigger Boss. He turned his car around and drove away.

Mike and Pedro and Tony all grinned.

"What a bulldozer does, can't be un-dozed," said Mike, with a wink.

Now when you drive along the new thruway you can see a little old house where the road swings a little to the right. Tall trees grow over it. A little old lady sits in front with her knitting. All over the doorway grow beautiful yellow roses.

"Oh, look at the roses!" people cry as they drive by. They slow down a little to look.

"Hum," says the little old lady to her cat, "they're not in such a hurry, after all."

256

# DADDIES

### By Janet Frank

What do Daddies do all day?
Daddies work while children play.

# They work at desks.

## They work in stores,

258

in factories

and out-of-doors.

# Daddies fix the clothes we wear.

Barber Daddies cut our hair.

Some Daddies help us keep well fed.
They make buns and cakes and bread.

Some catch fish for us to fry.

Dads make clocks

and Dads make chairs.

Farmer Dads grow corn and pears.

Dads are sailors dressed in blue.

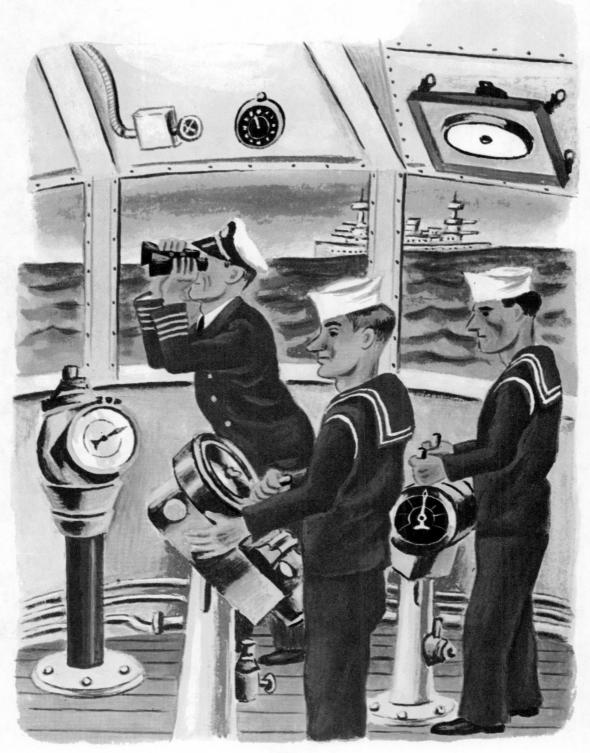

And Daddies are policemen, too.

Some Daddies mend our broken toys.

# And some teach little girls and boys.

Dads dig coal and Dads drive cars.
Dads put food in cans and jars.

Doctor Daddies keep folks well.
Daddies paint and Daddies sell.

Daddies sit at desks and write
the books we read in bed each night.

# Dads make steel

and Daddies sing.

Dads do almost everything.

But when they've worked
the whole day through
what do they like best to do?
By taxi, train, by car and bus,
Daddy rushes home—
to us!

# WHEEL ON THE CHIMNEY

## By Margaret Wise Brown

FIRST there was one stork.

Then there were two.

They had just arrived from Africa.

They built a nest on a wheel on top of a chimney.

They built in the spring when there was no smoke and the chimney would not be used again until winter.

First there was one stork, then there were two, soon there were four—the mother and father stork and two hungry babies with wide open beaks and white feathers.

The mother kept the little storks safe and warm under her wings while the father went out to get food for them.

Sometimes the father would keep them warm while the mother went fishing in the cool green rivers of Hungary.

Summer followed spring, cool and green. And the young storks grew longer legs. Their bills grew longer, but they never made a sound, for a stork is a silent bird.

The only sound he makes is the great clap-clapping of his beak.

In the olden days storks built nests on trees.

But it is considered a great honor to have a stork settle on your house—great honor and great good luck.

Some farmers bind cartwheels to the tops of their chimneys, or make platforms of twigs and straw, to invite the storks to land.

And while the other birds sing and the barnyard fowl cackle and crow and quack and hiss and cluck all through the long green summer, the storks are silent—silent and beautiful.

Then one day the air grew colder, and a black stork arrived from the wild forests to the North.

More and more storks, wild black ones and great white ones that built their nests on wheels on the chimneys of houses, flew down from the sky and into a great green field.

The time to go South had come.

The storks would all fly South for the winter.

How did they know, who had lived all summer on the wheel on the chimney?

Then silently in great white flight they flew over the towns of Europe.

Over rivers and bridges and far away, always to the South.

They flew to the edge of the blue Mediterranean Sea and headed across the sea to Africa.

279

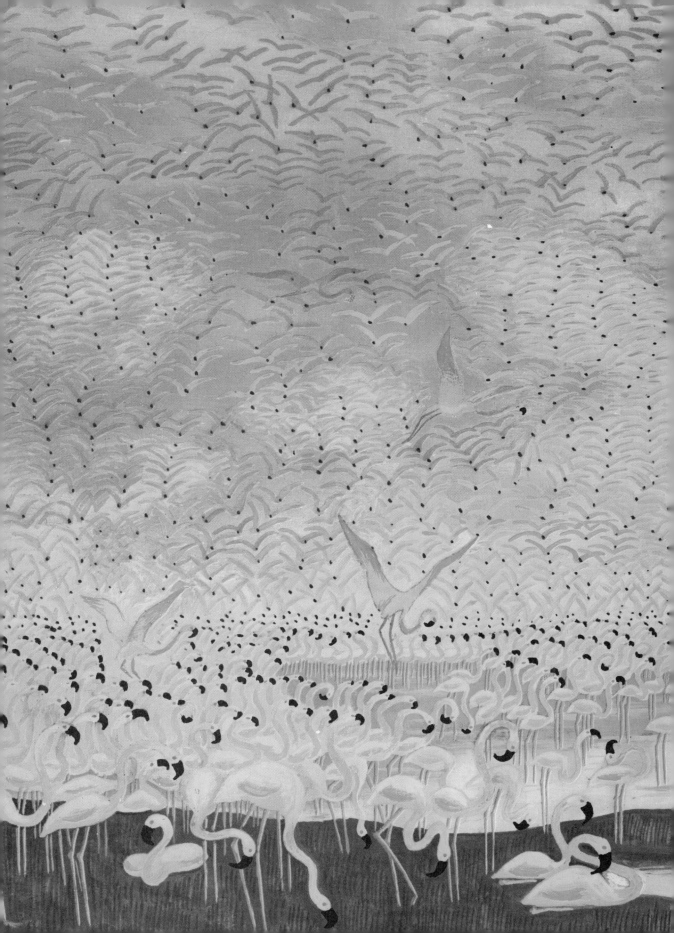

To the land of the Nile, where their cousins, great flocks of crimson flamingos the color of sunset, waded knee deep in the green waters of the river.

But they did not stop here—they flew on, high in the air to the South.

And here they lived for the winter—deep in the warm wild wilderness of Africa. And here where it was warm, they would stay until spring. And then one day great flocks of storks would gather and it would be time for the great flight to the North.

How did they know in that far-away land that spring had come in the lands of the North?

This is still a secret of the storks—North or South.

The wild black storks would fly with the white storks, though the black storks would fly further to the North than the white storks—into the great green forests —far from the farms of men where the white stork made his home.

Off they started up through the air to the North.

But a great storm shook the sky.

Golden lightning split the air and the storks were blown far out over the Indian Ocean, far off their course and away to the North.

One white stork was very tired. He was too tired.

So he collapsed onto the deck of a boat bound for Egypt.

When the captain saw that a weary stork had landed on his ship, he knew good luck had come his way.

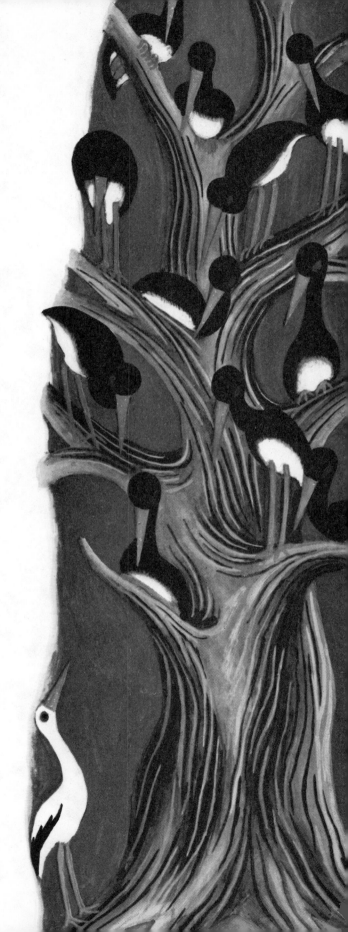

He gave the stork a great wicker chair like a nest to rest in. And he sent him French croissants and yellow tomatoes and good things to eat.

And the captain grew fond of the stork.

One day the stork flew away and the captain wished him a safe journey.

Over the jungles where the monkeys chattered and the baboons squealed, mid the shrill screech of the wild parrot and the pink cockatoo.

Over the wild green jungles he flew.

Snatched at by monkeys and screamed at by baboons.

At last he got out of the jungles by the strength of his brave white wings.

And soon he was over the wild still wastes of the Sahara Desert.

Then suddenly the silence of the sand was broken by an onrush of wings.

There were the other storks returning to the land of their birth.

And he flew with them over the desert towards the cool Northern spring.

Then one day in early spring there was the gentle rustle of birds building a nest of straw and twigs on top of the chimney.

The farmer had been expecting them.

He had tied a wheel on his chimney.

He knew storks are a sign of good luck to any house on which they choose to build.

First there were two
and then
spring had come
and the story starts all over again.

# THE
# LITTLE RED
# CABOOSE

*By Marian Potter*

The little red caboose
always came last.

First came the big black engine
puffing and chuffing.

Then came the boxcars,

then the oil cars,

then the coal cars,

then the flat cars.
Sometimes they were
switched around in different ways.

But the little red caboose
always came last.

Boys and girls waved
at the big black engine.

They listened to the boxcars
and the oil cars
and the coal cars
and the flat cars
go *clickety clack*.

But by the time the little red caboose
came along, the boys and girls
were turning away.
Because the little red caboose
always came last.

"Oh, smoke!" said the little red caboose.

"I wish I were a flat car
or a coal car or an oil car
or a boxcar, so boys and
girls would wave at me.

"How I wish I were a big black engine,
puffing and chuffing way up at the front of the train!

"But I'm just the little old red caboose.
Nobody cares for me."

One day the train started up a mountain.

Up went the big black engine.
Up went the boxcars.
Up went the oil cars.
Up went the coal cars.
Up went the flat cars.
Up went the little red caboose.

"Hang on tight, little caboose," called the flat car.
"This is a long tall mountain.
And you are the last car on the train."
"Don't I know it!"
sighed the little red caboose. "Poor me!"
The train went slower and slower and s-l-o-w-e-r.

Soon it was hardly moving.
It looked as if that train
could not get up the mountain.
"Look out, little caboose!"
called the flat car.
"The train is starting to slip
back down this long tall mountain!"

"Not if I can help it!"
said the little red caboose.
And he slammed on his brakes.
And he held tight to the tracks.
And he kept that train
from sliding down the mountain!

Then, *bump!*
The little red caboose felt
something push him from behind.
It was a big black engine.
No, it was two big engines!

They were in back
of the little red caboose, puffing and chuffing.
They pushed the train up to the top
of the mountain.

And they were the last cars
on the train!
"We couldn't have done it,"
said the big black engines,
"if it had not been for the
little red caboose."
Everyone cheered.

And the little red caboose
nearly burst with pride.

Since then, boys and girls
wave at the big black engine.

They listen to the boxcars
and the oil cars
and the coal cars
and the flat cars go *clickety clack*.

But they save their biggest waves
for the little red caboose,
because the little red caboose saved the train.

And the little red caboose comes last.

# ABOUT THE SEASHORE

## By Kathleen N. Daly

ALL around our world there are sea-shores. At the seashore, the waters of the sea meet the land.

There are many kinds of seashore. Some seashores are covered with sand, smooth and soft and good for digging,

308

and making sand pies, and moats and castles.

Other seashores are rough and rocky.

There may be steep cliffs, and dark caves for hiding in, and little secret bays, and big rocks for climbing.

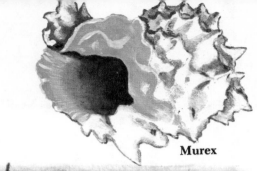

**Murex**

Some days big waves come rolling up to the seashore.

The wind helps to pile up the water into waves. The waves hit the shore with a roar and a crash and a cloud of spray.

There are many things to see on the seashore.

There are pretty pebbles to find. Some of them are flat and smooth and good to skip over the surface of the sea.

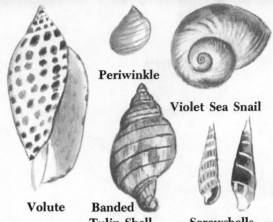

Volute

Periwinkle

Violet Sea Snail

Banded
Tulip Shell

Screwshells

Other pebbles are sharp, and some are shiny, or spotted, or striped.

There are shells on the seashore—pink shells, white shells, blue shells, shells of many colors.

These shells were once the homes of tiny animals of the sea.

Some shells are in one piece.

Other shells have two parts. They fit

together around the animals that made them.

In the shallow water near the shore live many creatures.

Some, like lobsters, swim and scurry around quickly. Others, like clams and snails, move very slowly. Some creatures, like barnacles, cling tightly to rocks and hardly move at all.

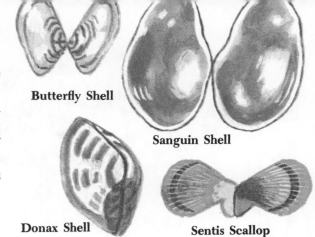

**Butterfly Shell**

**Sanguin Shell**

**Donax Shell**

**Sentis Scallop**

Lady Crab

Ghost Crab

Blue Crab

Mud Crab

Fiddler Crab

Horseshoe Crab

In the water and on the beach there may be crabs—big crabs, little crabs, middle-sized crabs. Their eyes are on little stalks, and they usually walk sideways.

Big horseshoe crabs are not true crabs. But they have shells, just as crabs do.

There are birds at the seashore.

Sandpipers run busily over the wet sand.

312

Herons wade in the shallow water.

Greedy pelicans watch for a chance to fill their pouches with fish.

Sea birds lay their eggs on the seashore. They may lay them in the sand.

Or they may nest on rocky ledges high above the water.

Beyond reach of the waves some plants grow.

Plants that grow near the sea have to be tough and sturdy. They have to stand against the strong sea winds and the salty spray.

The plants that grow in the water are

called seaweeds. Seaweeds may be red, or brown, or green.

Some float near the top of the water. Others hold fast to the bottom of the sea, or cling to the rocks near the shore.

Each day at the seashore there is a high tide and a low tide. At high tide the water comes far up the shore.

Then at low tide the water goes back down the shore again. The tide leaves pools and good-smelling seaweeds and shells behind it on the shore.

It is the moon that pulls the waters of the sea to make the tides.

There are exciting things to see in the pools left by the tide. There may be

314

a prickly sea urchin, or a starfish. Shells may be there, too, with the little animals that live inside them.

On cold, lonely seashores, seals come in from the ocean to have their babies.

Then the mother seals teach their pups to dive and swim and catch fish in the ice-cold water. Father seals keep watch over them all.

Mother sea turtles lumber up onto warmer shores to lay their eggs. They bury the eggs in the sand to keep them safe. Then they go back to the sea.

When the baby turtles hatch, they must find their way to the sea. It is often a long walk for tiny new turtles.

Busy people work along the seashores. Lobstermen tend their lobster pots.

Fishermen bring in their catch, and send it off to be sold in the markets.

Fishing nets have to be mended. Sometimes fishermen's wives and fishermen's children help with the mending.

Clam diggers hunt for clams.

At the edge of the sea there are places where boats may come to harm.

There are rocky ledges and bars of sand hidden under the water.

Lighthouses warn boats of danger. They help to make our seashores safe.

Along the seashore there are places where the water is quiet and deep.

These are good places for boats and ships to anchor safely.

These are harbors, and sometimes great cities grow up near them.

Harbors are busy places. Big ships set out to sail across the ocean. Cargo boats bring things from distant lands. Little ships move in and out among the big ones.

All around our world there are seashores, where the waters of the sea meet the land.

And all along the seashore there are exciting things to see and do.

# ANIMAL ORCHESTRA

## By Ilo Orleans

In Animal Town
It was Musical Day.
The orchestra
Had gathered to play.

Everyone came
To hear and to see.

The big sign said,
ADMISSION FREE!

Up to the platform
Each animal went,

And proudly carried
His instrument.

They whistled! They fiddled!
They thumped! They blew!

What a roar! What a din!
What a great to-do!

The animal girls—
The animal boys—
The animal audience
Made a great noise.

They slapped their tails,
They clapped their paws,
And that is how
They made applause!

The conductor bowed,
And bowed and bowed.
All of the orchestra
Players were proud.

The Hippo was happy
On Musical Day,
For everyone shouted,
*"Hip-HIPPO-ray!"*

# THE DEEP BLUE SEA

## By Bertha Morris Parker and Kathleen N. Daly

Oceans cover more than half of our earth. All the oceans together are sometimes called the sea.

There is more sea than land on this earth of ours. The sea is big and deep and full of exciting things to know about.

The surface of the sea looks flat. But underneath the sea there is a strange, dim world. There are valleys and hills, mountains and canyons, just as there are on the earth above.

There are valleys deeper than any we can imagine. Some of the mountains are higher than any on land. Some of them rise up above the waves, and appear as islands in the ocean.

The sea looks empty. But it is full of living things.

Almost everywhere, there are fish. Some swim near the surface of the sea.

Flying fish can leap right out of the water and glide through the air.

Bluefin Tuna

Grouper

Moorish Idol

Sergeant Majors

Angelfish

Blue-striped Snapper

Starfish

Butterfly Fish

Sea Horses

Flounders

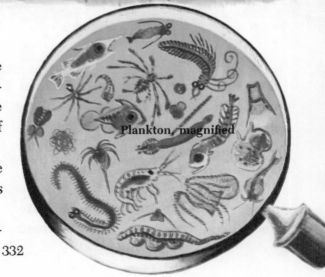

Plankton, magnified

There are hundreds of kinds of little fish, spotted and striped and bright colored. They dart in and out among the rocks and seaweeds in the gardens of the sea.

Some fish stay near the floor of the sea. The flat flounder is one, and its speckles help it to hide.

Some fish make long journeys. Some-

332

times they travel together in great crowds called schools.

At egg-laying time, a few travel back to the waters where they were born. No one knows how they find their way.

Even where there are no fish, the sea is not empty. Floating about in the sea are millions of tiny plants and animals. They are so tiny that human eyes cannot see them easily. All of them together are called plankton.

Many sea creatures feed upon plankton. It is a kind of sea soup for them.

Fish are always moving about. There are many dangers for them.

There are bigger, hungry fish. Some

Barracudas

Tiger Sharks

Remoras

Pilotfish

Cormorants

of the fiercest fish are the sharks and barracudas.

Fishermen set out in fishing boats and go far out to sea. Some places of the sea are especially good for catching fish. The fishermen go there and put down great nets for the fish to swim into. They catch whole boatloads of fish for people to eat.

Sea birds eat fish. Noisy gulls and graceful terns and cormorants all swoop and glide over the waves, watching for fish with their sharp eyes.

When a cormorant sees a fish, it closes its wings and dives deep down into the water to catch it.

Many birds fly far out to sea. They may ride for hours at a time on the

Blue Whale

Common Dolphin

Albatross

Arctic Terns

Murres

Blue-footed Booby

Gannets

strong sea winds. When they are tired, they may rest on the waves, or on a passing ship. The seas are great highways, and many ships travel back and forth across them.

The biggest animal in all the world lives in the sea. It is the whale. A whale is not a fish, and it cannot stay under water all the time. It must come up to the surface to get air.

When a whale spouts, it is blowing out stale air from its lungs.

Often there is a baby whale swimming beside its mother, and learning the ways of the sea.

Sometimes a whale floats lazily in the sun. A sea bird may rest on its head, and small fish swim in its shadow.

Long-snouted Dolphin

Harbor Porpoise

Rockweed
Trunkfish
Sargassum
Kelp
Irish Moss
Squirrelfish
Sargassum Fish
Spotted Chub
Sea Anemone
Sea Colander
Angelfish
Coralline Algae

Dolphins and porpoises are playful relatives of the whales.

There are plants in the sea.

Large brown kelps, feathery sea moss, green rockweed—all of these are seaweeds. Some seaweeds cling to rocks. Some float.

One part of the Atlantic Ocean is covered with floating seaweed. It is called the Sargasso Sea.

Squids, big and small, shoot through the waters of the sea. The eight-armed octopus is a relative of the squids. Sometimes it walks along the sea floor on its tentacles. When a squid or an octopus is attacked or frightened it can squirt out an inky cloud of liquid to hide itself.

Far down beneath the surface of the sea, deep deep down, the sea is dark. But even here, some fishes live.

Squids

Common Octopus

Blue Demoiselles

Dancing Octopus

Lobster

Starfish

Strange creatures they are. Some of them have long and terrible teeth, and some have glowing lights on their bodies.

Fierce, hungry fishes they are, and some can swallow fish much bigger than themselves.

The water of the sea is salty.

Rivers bring salt to the sea. Day by day, year by year, rivers gather salt from the rocks and carry it to the sea.

People sometimes collect salt from the sea.

Divers dive deep down into the sea to collect its treasures.

They look for oysters that have pearls inside their shells.

Or they dive down to a sunken ship. Sometimes divers help to bring back some of a ship's cargo.

The water of the sea is always moving, even when it looks still.

It moves in broad streams of water called currents.

Sea currents carry water from one part of the sea to another. The water in a current may be warmer or colder than the sea around it. It may be a different color, and look like a river in the sea.

The wind blowing on the sea makes the water pile up into waves.

Sometimes a strong wind will blow for many days, and form huge waves. They go rolling over the ocean, big and angry and frightening.

But when the winds are gentle, the sea is friendly. There are little waves to splash in, and playful breezes for sailboats.

The sea is big and deep and full of things to know about. The sea seems to be saying,

"Come travel on my waters, come explore me. Come learn my secrets."

# GERGELY'S GOLDEN CIRCUS

*By Peter Archer*

# SETTING UP THE BIG TOP

Eᴀʀʟʏ in the morning, the circus comes to town.

Its train rolls to a stop on the siding, and one-two-three, everyone is at work. Down from flat cars the circus wagons slide on ramps. Elephants are unloaded, and soon a parade of trucks and gaily painted wagons starts rolling over to the circus grounds.

There everything seems a hurly-burly. But the great tent city is steadily rising. First tent up is the cookhouse, for working with the circus is a hungry job. And last of all, the Big Top is ready to go up.

Up and up goes the enormous circle of canvas, opening like a giant umbrella, until it covers its towering masts. Then the "Big Top gang" anchors its guy ropes, and other crews hurry inside to get everything ready in time for the afternoon show.

341

# DRESSING UP

The troupers are busy getting ready for the show, too.

After breakfast, the clowns unpack their costumes and begin to paint on their funny faces and put on their costumes.

Water boys carry water for the animals, and the animal men begin to groom their charges.

The horses paw restlessly while they are being brushed and curried. The elephants sway gently while their skins are oiled and rubbed.

Tillie, queen of the herd, likes this so much that she blows a soft, reed-like hum through her trunk.

Soon all the other elephants are humming along with her.

# GROOMING THE ANIMALS

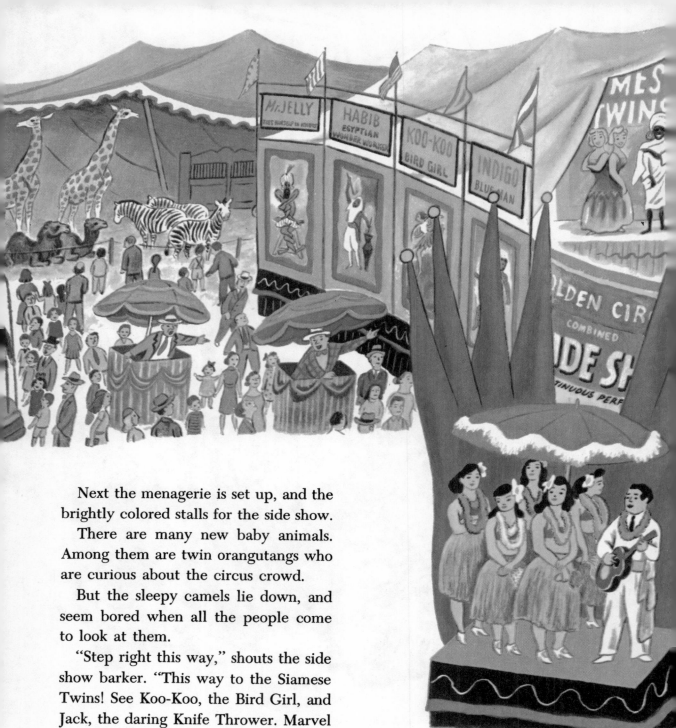

Next the menagerie is set up, and the brightly colored stalls for the side show.

There are many new baby animals. Among them are twin orangutangs who are curious about the circus crowd.

But the sleepy camels lie down, and seem bored when all the people come to look at them.

"Step right this way," shouts the side show barker. "This way to the Siamese Twins! See Koo-Koo, the Bird Girl, and Jack, the daring Knife Thrower. Marvel at the Human Skeleton, and Dotty Dimples, the fattest woman in the world—"

All the side show folk are pleased to hear how wonderful they are. Only the

SIDE SHOW AND

# MENAGERIE

Hindu Sword-Swallower doesn't smile. He sits wondering what the barker is saying, and waiting for a glimpse of the odd-looking people who come to stare at his act.

At last every seat in the towering grandstand is filled. People look down at the three rings and the blur of color below.

Just before show time, there is a moment of breathless silence. Then the Ringmaster blows his whistle. The band strikes up a march. And in sweeps the wonderful opening parade.

**GRAND**

Around the tanbark go prancing horses, magnificent elephants, solemn camels, gay little dogs strutting along. Along come the clowns, and glittering floats filled with beautiful ladies and fairy-story folk.

Row by row, the people stand up and shout for joy and surprise. Then they settle back to watch the show.

# MARCH

347

# THREE-RING CIRCUS

Now the band plays a fanfare, and suddenly all three rings are filled with tumblers, acrobats, and jugglers. Everyone is moving.

In one ring, the jugglers balance towering columns of ninepins on their heads,

or keep dozens of shining circles dancing in the air. In another, an acrobat bounces from a teeterboard, turns a back-flip in mid-air, and lands neatly in a chair on top of a pole ten feet high!

And in the center ring there is so much to watch that the audience cannot see it all at once! Clowns ride on funny bicycles, and a daring cyclist speeds around the ring while his partners leap on his shoulders and the sides of his swiftly moving bicycle.

# HORSES

As the acrobats leave the ring, the band sounds a trumpet-call and the horses come prancing in.

Some, ridden by master horsemen, go through their graceful steps in perfect time. They strut and dance around the ring. When the crowd claps in delight, the horses kneel in a low bow.

The "liberty" horses perform without riders. They drill to their master's quiet commands, and rear up with arched necks at the crack of his whips.

And the big bareback horses pace so smoothly that whole teams of trick riders can jump from one horse to another! Then beautiful ladies will dance on the horses' backs.

# BETWEEN

During intermission, the band plays its merriest music. The rings are empty and the lights seem dimmer.

The people stretch their legs, and talk about all the wonderful acts they have seen.

They buy good things to eat, too, and balloons and souvenirs to take home with them.

10¢

HOT DOG

15¢

CANDY

ICE CREAM

ORN

# THE ACTS

The clowns have as much fun as everyone else. They visit with the children in the audience and they play all sorts of silly games around the rings.

When the music ends, everyone claps so hard and loud that the bandleader beams with pride, and the musicians in their scarlet coats bow again and again.

# ELEPHANTS

Tramp, Tramp, Tramp! Here come the elephants, swaying trunk to tail.

Around the whole arena they march. Then up go their trunks, and gently they swing their riders to the ground. One of the lady riders kneels on an elephant's

neck while the great beast stands on its head.

Two elephants lean against a tub, and two others lie across them to form a great pyramid. And a beautiful lady balances on the trunk and head of the biggest elephant. At last Tillie, the oldest and wisest elephant of them all, swings her trunk high.

Then all the elephants rise on their hind legs for the "long mount," and the elephant act is over.

# PACKING UP

At last the wonderful circus is over. The happy crowd spills out into the circus grounds. And after the last performance in town, those grounds look strangely bare.

All during the show, the work crews

were quietly packing up. After each act, the animals and performers streamed back to the circus train. Now only the Big Top must be taken down and loaded aboard—and the biggest show on earth will be ready to move on.

# AND MOVING ON

357

# THE HAPPY
# LITTLE WHALE

*Told to Jane Werner Watson*
*by Kenneth Norris*

ONCE upon a time there was a little whale,
nine feet long from her nose to her tail.
She lived far out in the deep blue sea,
which for whales is a very fine place to be.
She and her playmates as a rule
traveled with a group of whales called a school.
Those little whales had lessons to learn.
They swam and they dove and they surfaced in turn
and they blew great fountains of watery spray
and talked in squeaks in a whalish way.

They even learned to stand on their tails,
which is a special trick of whales.
One day as the whole school swam along,
they saw a strange something which didn't belong.
It was a boat, not just out for a sail
but manned with fishermen looking for whale!

It didn't look fearsome, so our little whale stood
on her tail as close to the boat as she could.
Just then from the boat a net shot out,
and it covered our little whale round about!
She swam this way and that. She dove deep down.
She jumped toward the sky and rolled all around.

She sighed and she snorted and she blew a jet,
but she couldn't get free of that tangling net.
The rest of the whales all tried to help.
They swam through beds of weedy kelp.
They swam through stretches of open sea.
But they could not set that small whale free.
All through the night our little whale
fought that net that held her like a jail.
By morning she was tired out, fore and aft.
And just then under her there slid a rubber raft.

That raft stretched under the weary little whale
like a billowy bed from her head to her tail.
When the raft started moving in toward the shore
the other whales couldn't follow any more.
So they turned and swam out to sea,
and the little whale felt as lonely as could be.

She was falling off to sleep when, in a flash,
she was lifted up high and then landed with a splash
in the good salty water of a big round pool.

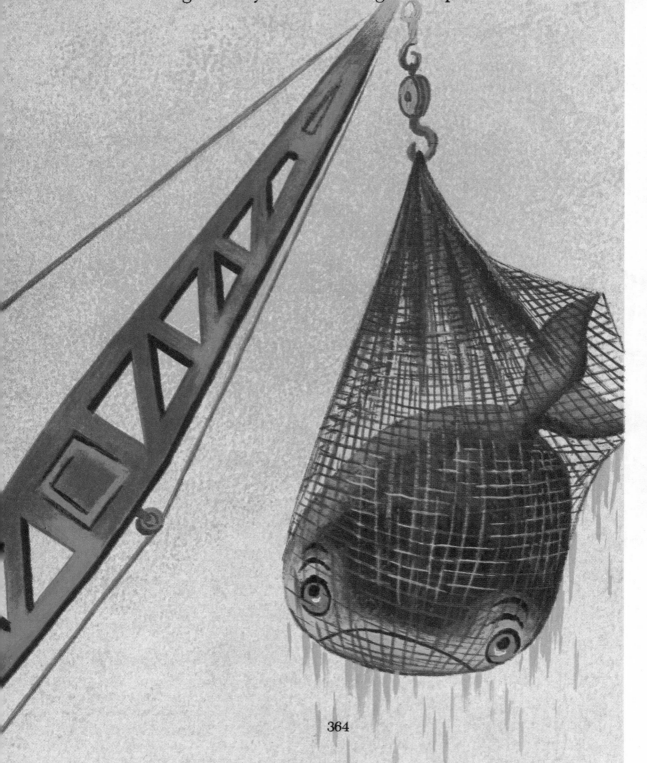

She swam around looking for her playmates
and the school,
but she couldn't find anyone. My oh me,
that poor little whale was as lonely as could be.

Then into the pool flipped a strange black fish,
and he swam right up to that little whale.
When she opened her mouth,
which was bigger than a pail,
in went a mouthful of tasty squid.
Little whale swallowed the squid quick quick!
She felt much better, but she wanted some more,

so she opened her mouth as she had before.
In went another mouthful of fish!
She gulped it right down, as fast as you could wish.
And she felt so fine when the meal was done
that she blew a whole fountain of spray, just for fun!

Well, that strange black fish kept bringing her squid,
and he taught that little whale tricks, yes he did.
He taught her to shake flippers when they'd meet
and to jump right out of the water for a treat.

He taught her to wear a fancy hat
and to jump through a hoop, and things like that.
One day little whale heard noises and shouts.
She wondered what all the excitement was about.

Soon they lifted her up with a great big crane
and set her down again, without any strain,
in a great big tank where she could swim around
and roll and splash and dive deep down.
And what should appear there before her eyes
but a little whale playmate just her size!

Now those two little whales are as happy in the pool
As they once had been in the deep-sea school.
They swim and they roll and blow spray
when they wish,
and they do all their tricks for treats of fish.

They wear fancy hats and shake flippers
with their friends
and they jump for fish, and when the show ends . . .
they sometimes stand right up on their tails
and squeak for joy, those two happy little whales!

# THE GOLDEN YEAR

*By Peggy Parish*

## JANUARY

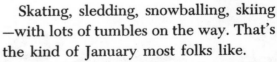

SHORT days, cold days, filled-with-winter-fun days. That's the month of January.

Snowsuits, boots, mittens, hats, scarves —such a bother. Bears' fur coats grow thicker in the winter to keep them warm, but some bears like to dress up anyway.

Skating, sledding, snowballing, skiing —with lots of tumbles on the way. That's the kind of January most folks like.

Are you lucky enough to live where there's lots of snow? Wouldn't it be nice if everybody did!

# FEBRUARY

FEBRUARY is the month for remembering. It is the month for remembering the important things Lincoln and Washington did. And best of all, it's the month for remembering the people we love. We send them valentines. Everyone in the Bear family got a valentine this year.

That occasional mild, sunny day in February helps us remember that spring will soon be here. But don't pack away your snowsuit. While February is the shortest month, it may also be the coldest. February is the month for remembering all sorts of things.

# MARCH

When the leaf of the oak is the size of a squirrel's ear, it's planting time. That's what the Indians of long ago said. And it's still true today. The melting snows change the earth to mud. The March winds help dry the earth, leaving it soft and damp and easy to dig.

How exciting it is to plant a tiny seed in the fresh earth! The Bear cubs can hardly wait to see the first green sprout come up.

And the bird is watching and waiting for a nice fat worm.

The animals who hibernated all through the winter begin to wake up. Spring is here at last!

375

# APRIL

IN APRIL the earth sparkles with new-ness and color. Bright pink peach blos-soms, pale pink apple blossoms, fluffy white plum blossoms—each blossom holds a promise of fruit to come.

Ladylike daffodils, giggly faced pan-sies, shy violets welcome the showers which April brings.

Forest, field, and barnyard become alive with new baby animals eager to find out about the world. And look! The Bear family has a new cub!

Houses wear new coats of paint, and families wear new spring clothes.

With a swish and a squiggle of the paint brush, even ordinary eggs become wonders of brightness. April is indeed a month of newness and color.

# MAY

In May, the outdoors is calling for you to come out. It's so hard to sit still and think about lessons. Trees are all leafed out and want you to climb. Butterflies flit by begging to be chased. Your toes wiggle when you think about walking barefoot in the new grass.

And there are so many things to find out. Is the brook warm enough for wading? Does the wild plum tree have many plums? Are the early berries ripe yet?

Bears and raccoons have their eyes on those berries, too. They are just as eager as you for that first juicy fruit.

But each day in May brings you closer to vacation. Just have a bit of patience.

# JUNE

EVERYBODY loves June! Vacation begins. The days are long and warm. And everybody is ready for fun.

June is a nice time to take a nature walk through the woods. Many wild flowers are in bloom. If you walk very quietly you will probably see some mother animals with their babies, too.

Fathers often take their families on trips in June. What fun it is to see new sights, to eat out, and to have your father with you all day. Do you suppose animal fathers take their families on vacation trips, too?

Remember Father's Day comes in June. And fathers like surprises, too.

# JULY

Hot! Hot! Hot! That's the month of July. This would be a good month to be a fish. But, if you're not, underneath a sprinkler or in a backyard pool is a nice place to be.

Independence Day is a holiday for almost everybody.

And it's never too hot for a family picnic with fried chicken, potato salad, lemonade, and ending with big slices of juicy, red watermelon.

Be sure to find out if there is a fireworks exhibition on the night of the Fourth. You wouldn't want to miss that!

379

# AUGUST

AUGUST is the last month of vacation, so make every minute count. Think back over your plans for the summer. Have you done everything you meant to do?

Bears and other animals that hibernate are very busy now. They are eating as much as they can. The fatter they get, the better it is for them. For then, they can sleep in a cozy den throughout the cold, cold weather and not get hungry. Their bodies will use the food they have stored as fat.

# SEPTEMBER

"SCHOOL DAYS, school days, dear old golden rule days."

How exciting that first day of school is! Seeing your old friends. Meeting new ones. Hearing all about your friends' vacations, and telling about yours.

Vacation time is nice, but when the leaves begin to turn, and there's a smell of fall in the air our thoughts turn to school. We're ready to get back to work.

And September begins that new school year. Aren't *you* glad to be back?

# OCTOBER

October is harvest time. And harvest time is busy time. Farmers hustle and bustle to get the crops in. Mice, squirrels, and chipmunks hurry and scurry to gather their winter food. Raccoons, skunks, and bears stuff themselves on the last fruits of the season.

October is dress-up time. The trees change their summer greens to brilliant reds, oranges, golds, and browns. And children dress-up for Halloween. Don't be surprised if your doorbell rings and you find a witch or a ghost or a dressed-up bear calling, "Trick or treat?"

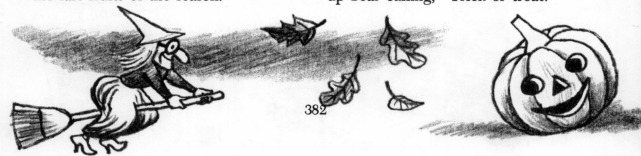

# NOVEMBER

NOVEMBER is a resting month. The trees are bare. The flowers have faded away. Nature has done her work for the year. It is time to rest.

The crops are gathered. The food is stored away. Farmers have done their work. It is time to rest.

When the first snowflakes fall, many kinds of animals nestle in their cozy dens. They are fat and contented and very sleepy. It is time to rest.

But November is also a month of feasting and thanks. As you get ready for your Thanksgiving dinner, remember to say, "thank-you," for all the good things we have in life.

# DECEMBER

EVERYBODY loves the merry, hustling, bustling excitement of December. It is the month of happy holidays. Some people celebrate Christmas. There are other people who celebrate Hanukkah.

But for everybody December is a month for remembering friends with cards or gifts.

December is the month of pleasant smells—spicy evergreens, burning candles, good things baking. It is the month for lovely sounds—bells jingling, people singing, organ chimes. It is the month for beautiful sights—decorated trees, colored lights, fancily wrapped packages. December is a happy month.